"Two rooms, please."

"I'm sorry, sir. All we have available is a single room."

Paul looked at Gwen. Then back at the reservation clerk. "We'll take it."

"Wait a minute." Gwen pulled Paul back a bit from the desk. "We can't sleep together...."

"Don't worry," he said, smiling before she had a chance to protest further. "You can have the bed. I'll take the chair."

"Uh..."

"Don't worry. I'll be a perfect, uh..."

"Gentleman?"

He pointed at her. "Yes."

Gwen wasn't worried—not about Paul, at least. She was tired from all the drinks and dancing. And she lacked a toothbrush. But before Paul got the key, the nice reservation man handed him two baskets filled with all kinds of necessities. Everything they'd need to get through the night...

Including two shiny condom packets.

Blaze™

Dear Reader,

Okay, let's get this out front—this book means a great deal to me. Even though I finished writing *Ms. Match* some time ago, I can't stop thinking about Paul and Gwen.

Since it's part of THE WRONG BED miniseries, the story started out on the light side, a frothy frolic, steamy and just plain fun. But Paul and Gwen soon let me know that they were complex people with things to accomplish. Not that they didn't have a sense of humor about it, because frankly, they cracked me up, but this was no quick ride to the end of the block. Their road had twists and turns and detours, not to mention the rest stops in the bedroom, the shower, the... Well, you get the picture.

You wouldn't think that landing in the wrong bed with the wrong man would be the best thing that could ever happen to Gwen, and vice versa. But then, isn't it always the tricks of fate, the missed exit, that send us to our greatest adventures?

Enjoy the trip!

Love,

Jo Leigh

JO LEIGH
Ms. Match

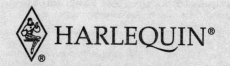

TORONTO • NEW YORK • LONDON
AMSTERDAM • PARIS • SYDNEY • HAMBURG
STOCKHOLM • ATHENS • TOKYO • MILAN • MADRID
PRAGUE • WARSAW • BUDAPEST • AUCKLAND

ISBN-13: 978-0-373-79428-7
ISBN-10:   0-373-79428-2

MS. MATCH

www.eHarlequin.com

Printed in U.S.A.

ABOUT THE AUTHOR

Jo Leigh has written more than forty novels for Harlequin and Silhouette Books since 1994. A triple RITA® Award finalist, she has contributed to many series, most recently Harlequin Blaze. Jo loves that she can write mysteries, suspense and comedies all under the Blaze banner, especially because the heart of each and every book is the love story.

Jo lives in Utah where she's hard at work on her next book. You can chat with her at her Web site, www.joleigh.com, and don't forget to check out her daily blog!

Books by Jo Leigh
HARLEQUIN BLAZE

*In Too Deep…
**Forbidden Fantasies
***Do Not Disturb

Don't miss any of our special offers. Write to us at the following address for information on our newest releases.

Harlequin Reader Service
U.S.: 3010 Walden Ave., P.O. Box 1325, Buffalo, NY 14269
Canadian: P.O. Box 609, Fort Erie, Ont. L2A 5X3

To Ryan, who (thankfully) knows his sports.

And no, he won't be allowed to read this book
till he's forty.

1

THE COFFEE SHOP was crowded as always just before seven, a long line of men and women dressed in what passed for business clothes in Beverly Hills snaking through the small round tables and out the door. Paul Bennet considered skipping his bagel and heading straight to the office, but he'd only had a couple of Dodger Dogs last night for dinner and he didn't like feeling hungry as he started his day. Not that kind of hungry at least.

Today would be a busy one. There was a new client on board, a television production company specializing in home improvement shows. They'd signed on to his public relations firm after being wooed by at least five other companies. But he'd done the final presentation pitch himself, and it had been a killer.

He bumped the arm of a young woman who glared up at him with fire in her eyes. The fire dimmed when he offered her a smile.

"Excuse me," she said, a slight blush coming to her cheeks.

"No problem."

She continued on her way and he silently urged the

line to speed up. He could wait and ask Tina, his secretary, to order in, but she wouldn't arrive till nine.

He liked to be the first in the office. In the quiet, he made his overseas and East Coast calls, went through his e-mail, did most of his real work. Once nine rolled around his day turned into a schmoozefest. He shouldn't complain. It was what he did best, the reason Bennet, Inc. was a success.

This morning, however, his first call would be to one Autumn Christopher. She would be in her hotel by now, relaxing with a drink and enjoying the view of the Piazza di Spagna.

He pictured her in her red-hot flight attendant uniform, with her long, blond hair pinned up primly. Her lips would match, scarlet and moist, but there would be no trace on her glass due to some feminine magic. That was only one of the ways she made him crazy. Like her smoky eyes when they looked him over from the ground up. The sound of her laughter. The fact that no matter what he did, no matter how charming, how lavish, how certain he was that he was on the mark, she simply wouldn't sleep with him.

The woman was no dummy.

He'd always been intrigued by the chase. Up to a point. Autumn had streaked past that point into territories hitherto unknown. Why then was he still after her? By now, hell, months ago, he should have kissed her off and pursued other opportunities. There was a world of women out there, and being in Los Angeles meant a world of extraordinarily beautiful women, so what was the deal?

Finally, he reached the counter. He pulled out his

smile once more, registering, barely, the response of the girl behind the counter. She blushed, glanced down, shuffled from side to side.

"Hi, Carol. I'd like an onion bagel, light cream cheese. Coffee, black. And I'd be delighted if you could add a smile to that order."

Despite the fact that he used the same silly line every time he got a bagel, Carol always reacted. Flushed, flustered and yet she always hustled for him, which was the ultimate goal. He didn't care for standing in line.

Quicker than it should have been possible, she returned with his order. "I put the bagel on the heat when I saw you two down," she said, her voice just loud enough for him to hear.

"That's what I love about you, Carol," he said, handing her a ten, which included a generous tip. "You're a treasure."

She sniffed and touched her hair. "Thanks, Mr. Bennet."

"I'll see you soon."

He was out of there in two minutes and into the building proper. He leased an entire floor of the high-rise. The lower floors were mostly concerned with banking, but the upper reaches had a number of offices that were unique to the area. Movie production companies, advertising firms that catered to the movie business, a casting office, two accounting firms that handled motion picture clients. It was showbiz all the way up here. His firm, for example, handled stars, film equipment firms, production companies, one of the smaller studios and three different commercial houses. They also had some sports clients, a few publishing companies and five, no six, authors.

He opened the doors to the front office, decorated to the nines by a leading Hollywood set designer. The artwork alone had cost him more than he'd earned his first two years in the business. The space smelled of the fresh flowers that were delivered weekly and that indescribable scent of money. Nothing about his business came cheap, which was the way he liked things.

He carried his bagel and coffee down the hall to his office. Here, on the twentieth floor, he was rewarded with a phenomenal view of the city. From Rodeo Drive to the Hollywood Hills, on a clear day it was the picture of fine living. Sadly, there weren't all that many clear days.

He sat behind his desk and turned on his computer. As he ate, he scanned his e-mails. Several needed quick responses, but most of them could wait. He was careful about his response timing. His clients tended to get greedy if he jumped on their queries.

A few minutes later, fortified by his admittedly meager breakfast, he slipped on his Bluetooth and rang up Autumn's cell phone. Three rings, then her lovely, soft, "Hello."

"Hey, beautiful."

"Paul," she said, and in that single word, she said everything. She was glad to hear his voice, pleased he'd called her beautiful and a little too delighted that it had all been on her terms.

"How's Rome?"

"Hot."

"Poor thing."

"It's not so bad. There's a pool in the hotel. I was about to get into my suit."

"Suit? Isn't that a bit of a stretch? That bikini of yours is no bigger than four Post-it notes."

She laughed, and just as it always did, the sound made his dick twitch.

"I know exactly what you should do," he said. "Use the video on your cell. Let me watch you strip."

Autumn sighed. "I have to hand it to you, Paul. You don't give up easily."

"Damn right I don't."

"I like that. I do. But I need to change the subject."

"Oh?"

"I have a favor to ask you."

He hoped it involved lingerie and champagne. "Ask away." He swung his chair around so he could view the city, the worker bees swarming to the hive. In New York, most everyone wore black. Dreary, even if the clothes themselves were daring. Not so in the City of Angels. It was warm today, and the colors on the people were as vibrant as the flowers lining Rodeo Drive.

"My parents are celebrating their fiftieth anniversary on Friday," Autumn said. "Only I'm going to be here."

"Okay," he said, his attention back on the conversation.

"The thing is, my sister doesn't have a date."

"Your sister."

"Uh-huh. Gwen. She says she doesn't care about going solo, but I know it's not true. I was wondering…"

"If she's anything like you, I'd be honored to be her escort."

Autumn laughed again. "No, not you. But you've got to know someone who wouldn't mind."

"Mind? Why would they mind?"

She sighed, one of those frustration deals complete with sound. "I don't want to be mean or anything, but Gwen's not exactly… She's very smart."

"Ah. She has a good personality."

"Exactly."

"How good?"

"She's not a troll or anything, but, well, you know. On the plus side, people seem to think she's interesting and funny."

"Got it. Not a problem. I have just the guy in mind. What's her number?"

"Don't have him call. Tell him to show up at her apartment. I'll let her know to expect him. Oh, and it's formal."

Autumn gave him the address and the rest of the details. He jotted it all down dutifully, even as he was busy counting the points he would earn for doing this little favor. He'd come through for her with shining colors. She'd have to say thanks. He could think of a hundred ways.

"You're a sweetie pie, Paul. I mean it. The anniversary party is a big deal. Thank you."

"I haven't done anything yet."

"You will. You were the first person I thought of to help out."

"Good. That's the way it should be."

She laughed, and somehow he knew the conversation was over, that there would be no video message sent to his phone, no more teasing on the international call. That was how Autumn did things.

"I've got to go if I'm going to catch that swim."

"When are you coming back?"

"Sunday."

"Can't wait," he said, and he knew that any other woman would have melted to those words, but not her. Not Autumn.

FOUR-FORTY ON FRIDAY afternoon and the office was shifting down to first gear. Paul had finished his last call ten minutes ago, and was now jotting down notes for the week to follow. He was looking forward to the evening. He had his monthly poker game, something he relished. No women were involved, only beer, fine cigars and the kind of raucous bullshit that could only come from a bunch of guys who'd known each other since college.

When Sam Ensler stepped inside his office, Paul's happy buzz died a quick death.

"Don't do this to me, Sam."

"You know I wouldn't if I had a choice."

"The party is tonight."

Sam, his go-to man in charge of literary PR, seemed miserable. He always looked kind of miserable, hence his nickname of Eeyore, but even Paul could see this was serious.

"I've got to go to Michigan," Sam said. "My mother broke her hip. She's having surgery in the morning."

"Shit."

Sam nodded. "There's no one else. She's eighty-five."

"I understand. Go take care of her. Take the time you need."

"I'm really sorry, Paul."

"No problem. What time was Gwen expecting you?"

"Seven." He put a piece of paper on Paul's desk. "That's her address."

"Got it," he said, his mind already racing through his list of friends and even acquaintances who could step in. "Let me know how your mother's doing, huh? And leave your cell on."

Sam smiled grimly as he turned to leave.

The minute he was alone, Paul cursed, vehemently. He had no idea who he could get for this gig on such short notice. Woody? No, Woody was in New York. Maybe Jeff… Shit. Jeff wasn't about to give up a Friday night to go out with an unattractive stranger. Who was he kidding? None of his friends would. Paul's only hope had been finding someone who either worked for him or who owed him. That second group should have given him a number of options. Except that it was a Friday night and there was just no time.

Cursing again, Paul dialed Cary's number. He got the voice mail, and left the message that he wouldn't make it to poker. Then he checked out Gwen Christopher's address. She lived in Pasadena. He'd have to get it in gear if he wanted to be on time. Thank God he always had at least one tux at the ready.

Autumn was going to owe him big-time.

HOLY SHIT. He was stunning.

Tall, unruly dark hair, stunning dark eyes, features that one would expect to see on the cover of *GQ*. He was one of the best-looking men Gwen Christopher had ever seen in person. Poor guy. He still hadn't gotten into Autumn's pants. It was the only reason Gwen could think of that a man who looked like him would agree to be her escort. "It's not going to work."

"Pardon me?"

She held the door open for him to come in. "Cinderella's not going to sleep with you because you're taking the ugly stepsister to the ball. She'll still make you wait."

The dazzling man blinked in charming confusion. "I'm not—"

She sighed as she closed the door. "I appreciate that you got all dressed up, so I'll make it easy for you. I'll tell Autumn you were perfect, a fabulous date. And I'll even give you a tip. She won't want you until you don't want her. Then her legs will part like the Red Sea. The night's young, and if you hurry, you can still make it to a premiere or whatever beautiful people normally do on a Friday night."

"Hey, lady, I'm just here to see if you want a copy of the *Watchtower.*"

Gwen laughed out loud, amazed that someone Autumn knew actually had a sense of humor. "Very good. It's Sam, isn't it?"

"No, actually it's Paul. Paul Bennet. I'm Sam's pinch hitter. He had to leave town. His mother broke her hip."

"Ah, well, then this really is your lucky night. Seriously, you don't need to stay."

"I didn't need to come. But I'd still like to take you to the party."

"Trust me. You don't."

Paul leaned back slightly and cocked his right brow, which made him even better looking. "Okay, so you really are Autumn's sister."

"What do you mean?"

"Stubborn." He took a step toward her. "I haven't got a single thing to do tonight. I'm dressed for the part. And I wouldn't mind checking out the rest of the family."

Wouldn't her whole clan just die when she walked in with Paul Bennet on her arm? It wouldn't last—a heartbeat after the shock wore off they'd all figure out that he was a mercy date. Still, it would be fun to see Faith with her perfect little mouth agape. "I've given you the secret to getting Autumn into bed. Don't you believe me?"

"I prefer to reach my own conclusions. What do you say then?"

"I say you're nuts."

"That's probably true. On the other hand, I was promised an open bar and a great buffet."

"Okay, I'll give you that. Honestly, there's not enough booze in the world to make this a delightful evening."

"I'll take my chances."

She looked at him, taken aback once more at how damn gorgeous he was. It was ridiculous, really. No one person should be allowed all that beauty. But then, beauty wasn't fair at all, was it? There was no doubt in her mind that she should put a stop to this madness right now. The whole situation was ludicrous. Could she actually be considering going to the party with this Adonis?

"Good, it's settled. Get your bag, Gwen. Let's go have some fun."

Even as she shook her head, she walked over to the dining-room table to pick up her purse. And when he held out his arm for her, she took it. It didn't surprise her that he had a shiny black Mercedes. But it did surprise her that she felt a little shiver in her tummy as he helped her inside.

PAUL SETTLED THE CAR onto the freeway and stole a glance at his companion. Autumn had exaggerated her sister's unattractiveness. She wasn't in Autumn's league, no, but she wasn't hideous, not by a long shot. Gwen was what he would consider plain. Nondescript eyes, a nose that could benefit from a good cosmetic surgeon, a too-broad jaw. Her body was nice, although bigger than most of his women friends. She carried herself confidently and put herself together well. But frankly, if he'd seen her at a party he'd have walked by without a second glance. It wasn't noble. Then again, he'd never claimed to be a paragon of virtue. He liked beautiful things. Cars, clothes, women. It wasn't a crime.

"So how do you know her?" Gwen asked.

"I met Autumn at a party for one of my author clients."

"Autumn knows an author? Autumn knows how to read?"

"I don't believe she knew him," he said, choosing to ignore the dig. "She was there as someone's guest."

"You can understand my confusion. She's not exactly a charter member of the book of the month club."

He smiled, thinking Gwen was right. "She has other charms."

"Yes, I suppose she does."

"You two aren't close?"

"No. Her circles and mine seldom intersect."

"So tell me about your circles."

She turned a bit to look at him and he felt as if he should have brought his college diploma to show her. "I'm a headhunter for Rockland-Stewart. Mostly scientific positions."

"Really? I've used a headhunter once or twice."

"For…?"

"Public relations. Primarily in the entertainment field."

She nodded. "That makes sense."

"Why?"

She went back to staring at the road. "You seem the entertainment industry type."

"Do I hear a note of disdain?"

"No, I'm sure it's fascinating work."

"Actually, it is."

"Why PR?"

"Why not? I'm good at it."

"That, I'm sure of. You were quite smooth stepping into this awkward position."

"So you would have preferred the original arrangement? Sam is a pretty interesting guy."

Gwen sighed. "I'm being horrible, I'm sorry. My sister believes she's doing me a favor, setting me up like this. I've told her at least a dozen times, if I wanted a date, I'd bring a date."

"You like going stag? Even to something like this?" Paul got over to the right lane, ready for the interchange. The party was at the Marriott in Burbank. It wasn't a long trip from her place in Pasadena, not by L.A. standards.

"It depends."

"On?"

She gave him a look that he couldn't make out as

most of her face was in shadow. "My sister and most of my family don't have a clue about my life. Just as I don't have much of a clue about theirs. It's just easier to go to family gatherings alone."

"I see."

"There's a chance you'll enjoy yourself, though," she said. "It'll be packed. Aside from all my parents' friends, there's my incredibly gigantic family. You know there are eight of us kids. Five of them are married and Faith is engaged. That's not counting their children."

"Whoa. I had no idea."

"All of them are more like Autumn than me. It was a joke my whole life that my mother had an affair with the postman."

"Unique is good."

"And there's the PR maven at work."

Despite the fact that Gwen was right, he wasn't liking this. Not even a little. Come on, he was doing a favor here. A rather large one. She could at least be gracious about it.

"I'm sorry. There I go again. It's nothing personal, I assure you," Gwen said.

"No problem."

"It is. You're doing a nice thing, even if your motivation is less than pure."

"Okay, I'm not a saint, but I still think we could make the best of it. If it will make you more comfortable, I can drop you off and arrange for a car to take you home when you're ready."

That seemed to startle her. She looked his way, although since he was exiting the freeway, he couldn't spare her much of a glance. It wasn't until they were at the first stoplight that she answered.

"I'll leave that to you. Have yourself a drink and something to eat. Leave when you feel like it. And you don't have to worry about a car home. I can take care of that, myself."

"Fine. Let's see how it goes."

Even though he couldn't really see her, he felt her relax. His own shoulders loosened, as well. Now that he had a tidy out, he figured if he played his cards right, he might still be able to make his poker game. He smiled as he turned into the Marriott driveway.

2

THE MOMENT the elevator door opened, Gwen heard a swing orchestra and knew her parents were in their version of heaven. They were both in their early seventies, but they still loved a great bash. That's why, in Gwen's solitary opinion, they'd had so many kids. They lived for an audience and a big dance floor. In their day they had been extraordinary dancers, winners of all kinds of prizes. When they got into the groove, they could outlast a lot of younger couples.

Gwen glanced at Paul as they made their way to the grand ballroom. He wore his tuxedo the way some men wear Levi's, as if it was the first thing he'd grab in the event of a fire.

Everything about him was the kind of slick you had to look for. So subtle that the signs of effort could easily be missed. His nails had been buffed, though not excessively so. His hair was perfectly mussed as if he'd just rolled out of a movie bed. Not a real bed, because that would be too risky, plus there was the whole eye-gunk and bad breath thing to deal with. No, Paul looked like a big-screen leading man.

Seconds before they reached the entrance, Gwen

thought about stepping closer to him, making sure her family and their friends would know that he was with her. The thought brought a wry grin to her face which she hoped Paul didn't see, or wouldn't know how to interpret.

She kept the same distance from him as they rounded the door, then felt his open palm on the small of her back.

Startled, she looked up at him. He smiled and gave her a wink, which would have been delightful if the underlying reason for his attention hadn't been pity. Despite those momentary urges to thumb her nose at her family, this was not the way she wanted to play. The game itself made her ashamed of her entire brood, and herself. She stepped away, dislodging his hand and any notion he might have harbored that she needed rescuing.

Paul took the rejection in stride, his seductive smile not faltering. It occurred to Gwen that the seduction was all part of his package. His personal autosetting. Seduce and conquer. Of course he was successful. He'd been born for his work.

"Gwen?"

She slowed at the sound of her sister's voice. Faith. Six years older than Gwen, Faith was a buyer for Neiman Marcus. Her fiancé, Bret, standing at her side, was also a buyer. The two of them were a match made in heaven. Between them, they almost had a whole brain. "Yes, Faith, it's me. Gwen."

"And who's this?" Faith eyed Paul as if he were a hot new designer jacket. Her whole face lit up with curiosity, which naturally made her even more beautiful. Her sisters, all five of them, had been models at some

time during their lives. Despite the fact that Faith was
thirty-four, she still fielded offers from photographers.

"Paul Bennet, my sister, Faith."

Paul bowed his head which made Faith sigh before
she looked back at Gwen. "You must give me the name
of the escort service. Not for me, naturally, but I know
a lot of women... Anyway, it's lovely to meet you."

Gwen's gaze shifted to Paul, catching the tail end of
his shock. He regained his aplomb quickly.

"I see the bar." He nodded toward the side of the
room and completely ignored Faith and her idiotic state-
ment. "Shall we get a drink?"

"I'd like that." Gwen took his arm and they headed
deeper into enemy territory. She thought about apologizing for Faith, but if she started down that road, she'd be
apologizing the whole night. Screw it. She'd have a drink,
see Paul off, then call a cab. It would be over before she
knew it, and she could forget all this nonsense.

The orchestra was fabulous. The music was all the
stuff she'd grown up with. Swing, mostly, with some old
standards thrown in for downtimes. She hadn't spotted
her parents yet, but there was Danny and his wife,
Sandy. And her sisters, Bethany and Eve.

Paul slowed as they reached the end of the line for
the bar. "What would you like?"

"Gin and tonic, please."

"No champagne?"

"Nope. To get through this night I need major fortification. In fact, make that a double."

"Sounds very wise," he said. "So how many of them
are out there?"

She knew without asking exactly what he was talking about. "All six. Plus six mates."

"Where do you fit in?"

She almost said she didn't. "It's Jess and Autumn after me. Everyone else is older, if not wiser. As I said, feel free to leave. I'm used to them."

"I don't know. That buffet looks great."

"I'm sure it is. My folks know how to throw a party."

He looked across the huge ballroom toward the orchestra. "I can see that. Do you dance?"

"We all learned. My parents were semipro when they were younger. We listened to swing bands instead of lullabies."

"I had to go to a dance academy. What a nightmare. I got beaten up regularly, and no, learning to fox-trot didn't help me become so light on my feet I came away unscathed. I had a permanent black eye until I was fifteen."

"But are you happy now?"

"Well sure. I haven't had a black eye in years."

She grinned. "I mean about the dancing."

"Ah. I suppose it's good to know how, although there are remarkably few opportunities to use the skills these days."

"That's true. And sad."

"There are some swing clubs in the Valley."

The woman standing in front of Paul turned to stare at him. Paul coughed. "Swing *dance* clubs," he said. "Although I'm pretty certain there are the other kind, too."

The woman who'd looked at him was one of her parents' golfing friends. They belonged to a club that cost a fortune and spent their days playing cards, tennis, even some lawn bowling. She was glad for them, that they had the money to live a leisurely retirement.

"Gwen, it's so nice to see you. It's been ages."

What the hell was her name? It was Bitsy or Kiki or some other silly thing, but Gwen couldn't recall. It didn't matter, though, as what's-her-name couldn't take her eyes off Paul. "Nice to see you, too. This is Paul Bennet, a friend of Autumn's."

The woman nodded as if it all suddenly made sense. "Where is that sister of yours?"

"Rome."

"Lucky duck. Rome is beautiful this time of year, don't you think?"

Paul slid a glance at Gwen. "I'm sure Autumn would prefer to be here."

"Oh, of course she would."

Paul stepped closer, very close, although he didn't touch Gwen. "My thoughts exactly."

With a final somewhat bewildered smile, the woman turned away, leaving Gwen yearning for her drink and her escape.

"Is it all parties you dislike so much, or just family parties?" Though his voice was low, considering the noise in the room, she heard him. Felt his warm breath on the side of her neck.

"I prefer small gatherings. With lots of conversation and laughter. Ah, finally."

They had gotten to the bartender at last. Paul ordered their drinks, and once they had them, she sipped as she led him toward the buffet. It was a huge spread, complete with an ice sculpture swan. Oysters on the half shell, colossal shrimp, crab legs, caviar. Everything was perfectly presented, the waitstaff attentive and polite. If only she could relax and enjoy herself. She juggled her glass and her plate until she had enough food to help ward off real drunkenness, then headed toward the far end of the ballroom where there were a few places to sit.

Paul found them two seats, and they joined a group of strangers. Gwen recognized some of them, but she had no names to go with the faces. It was nice, though, because the food and drink made chitchat difficult. She wondered if she should tell him again that he was free to leave, or if that would sound as if she was throwing him out.

"That's got to be one of the sisters," Paul said.

She followed his gaze to the outskirts of the dance floor. Bethany, the only sister Gwen was remotely close to, stood with her husband, Harry. They both looked gorgeous. Beth wore a long, shimmering silver dress that hugged her perfect figure. "That's Bethany. Husband Harry. They have a girl, Nickie, who's almost a year old."

"Another one?" He nodded toward the front entrance.

"Yep. That's Eve. Although I don't see the rest of her brood."

"I don't think I can pick out any of the brothers."

She glanced through the crowd, but she couldn't find any of the boys, either. "I'll point them out if they pass."

"What was it like to grow up with so many siblings?"

"It was great when I was very young. Not so much later on. The competition was fierce."

"Competition?"

"Unlike those delightfully cheery big families on television, our gang was all about points. Major points for football glory, modeling contracts, cheerleading squads."

"What about academics?"

She waved her hand, the shrimp she held bobbing. "No one actually discouraged getting good grades. But report cards weren't important currency. What about you?"

"There was pressure, most of it about grades. It was just me and my sister, Val. She's three years younger, and damn smart. Scary smart. Me, I had to bust my ass."

"You did well?"

"Yeah. I got into Yale, and they didn't throw me out for a fraud. I studied prelaw, but much to the disappointment of my father, it wasn't for me."

"You're lucky. You found your calling."

"I am."

She finished up the rest of her meal, digesting the fact that leading man Bennet had graduated from Yale. She probably should feel embarrassed at her own prejudice. In her experience men who looked like Paul didn't go Ivy League. Her brothers had done quite well in life having attended middling colleges. They'd understood early that charm and beauty opened more doors than prestigious degrees.

"Is there something else you'd like? More shrimp? Another drink?"

"No, I'm fine for now, thanks."

He stood up and she relaxed, knowing she would be free to leave soon herself. Paul held out his hand. Instead of a quick goodbye, he urged her to her feet. "Dance with me?"

"Oh. No. I—"

"Years of black eyes."

She knew that breathtaking smile wasn't really for her. It was all part of the game. What she couldn't understand was what he was doing with Autumn? Yes, she was stunning, a knockout. But she was also dumb as a post. Gwen laughed at herself. Didn't beauty trump smarts every time?

He tugged at her again, and she relented. It had to be the gin, that's all. Surely she wasn't fooled by his PR magnetism. As they went toward the dance floor, she looked down at her dress. She'd spent way too much on the damn thing, especially knowing she'd probably never wear it again. Still, when she'd tried it on, she'd felt so pretty.

She'd seen the dress in the window of a small Beverly Hills boutique and tried it on for a lark. How it fit her size-ten body made her feel more like a size two. So she'd closed her eyes to the outrageous price and excused her excess as a celebration in honor of a major win by her beloved Dodgers.

Finally, she would get to take the dress out for a spin. What did it matter if she danced with a pity date? She was allowed to have fun, dammit. Even here. Even with him.

PAUL KEPT HOLD OF HER HAND until they were in the middle of the crowded dance floor, afraid she'd try to escape if he let go. When he spun her into his arms, he was shocked to find her smiling. Not that tight, barely tolerant smirk she'd worn earlier tonight, but a real honest-to-god grin.

The orchestra broke into "Go Daddy-O," and Paul

got her ready. Gwen gave him a nod, and the two of them were off.

He hadn't danced like this in years, since that brief swing craze had made the rounds. But it all was there, right next to his fox-trots and waltzes and sambas.

It helped that Gwen kicked ass.

Unlike almost every woman he'd danced with since grammar school, she knew how to follow. She could actually read his hand as he guided her, his feet before they made a move. If they hadn't been wearing evening clothes, he'd have really let loose. He knew she'd love it if he swung her into the air or into a deep slide between his legs.

No matter, this was still exhilarating. Not as good as bed-busting sex, but it would do.

As he pulled her into a twirl, her head went back and she laughed out loud, a sound that made him laugh himself, just for the hell of it.

The whole thing was crazy. Dancing like a madman, dancing with Gwen. Enjoying himself so much he just might not leave after this song. One more wouldn't hurt. The poker game would still be going if he stayed for a couple more numbers.

By the time this song ended he was sweating a bit, not completely winded thanks to his workout routine, yet he needed a minute. From the look of things, Gwen did, too. He could tell from her dancing that she was in good shape. It was odd. He'd never gone out with athletic women. Most of his dates were thin. Well, skinny. He liked the models, liked how they looked on his arm. They had never really wanted to do much. Of course, they never ate, at least not in front of him.

"That was wonderful." Gwen fluttered her long dress, trying to cool down. "You're really good."

"It was worth the beatings, then?"

"I'd say so."

"Drink first? Or wait to hear what they play next?"

Just then the band lit up the stage. Paul didn't recognize the tune, but he sure got the beat. He grabbed Gwen and they did it so right they cleared half the floor.

They were both breathing hard after that number, and Gwen dragged him to the bar. She got water and another double, and he saw no reason not to do the same. Just as he'd finished his water, one of the sisters, Eve, showed up in front of them, her focus solely on Paul.

"I saw you dancing," she said as she did a full body inspection. "How on earth did Gwen find you? Don't tell me he's one of your famous bar buddies."

The question itself could have been harmless, but it wasn't. Second sister, second dig. He glanced at Gwen and caught her midsigh before she took a healthy swig of her gin and tonic.

"He was a free gift with purchase. Gotta love those coupons."

Paul took a step toward his date and put his hand on her back as he smiled brightly.

Only then did Eve look at her sister. Jesus, what the hell was it with this family? At least Autumn had been marginally complimentary about Gwen. Eve's expression left no room for misinterpretation. She found Gwen distasteful. There had to be more to this twisted dynamic than looks.

He had a lot of experience with the subject. He'd won and lost friends over his looks and he personally set his standards very high, but he saw no reason to be so out-and-out rude about it. He half turned his back on Eve and smiled. "You ready for the next round?"

Gwen put her almost-empty glass on a drink tray. He downed the rest of his own, and they were off, leaving Eve without another glance.

This time, it was a samba, a juicy Latin rhythm, and once again Gwen was the perfect partner. The real surprise came about an hour later, after another round of drinks, when the orchestra decided to give the crowd a breather and some songs that weren't meant to show off anything but how close two people could get and still keep it legal.

Paul didn't think twice about pulling Gwen into his arms. He liked the feel of her there, the way she antici-pated his moves. As he got a whiff of her perfume, sweet and smoky despite the workout she'd had, he wondered if she'd be just as responsive in bed.

"What's the matter?"

He looked down at her. "What?"

"You stopped. Is something wrong?"

Shit. He started moving again, smile pasted on as he swayed to the music. After a few minutes he didn't have to worry about the smile, or his thoughts. Of course he'd thought about her in bed. He was a man. She was a woman. Dancing was intimate work. It was all in the same genre, so to speak. It wasn't a big thing. In fact, it wasn't a thing at all.

It still wasn't a thing later when he noticed the ballroom was half-empty. That the buffet was serving coffee and pastries. The night had gone by in a whirl of drinking and dancing. At some point, he'd met Gwen's parents, and a few other brothers and sisters, all of whom made some kind of crack about him being her date, but mostly, they'd danced until they had to sit.

Each break, they sat farther away from the music and the crowds. She'd find the table, he'd bring the drinks and once he discovered she was also a rabid Dodger fan, the evening transformed yet again.

He'd have never guessed it could be so easy to talk to a woman when flirting wasn't on the table. He'd met a lot of women who didn't interest him that way, but he rarely spent a lot of time with anyone where there wasn't an agenda. Tonight, he was off the hook. He was earning his points with Autumn, sure, but there really was no pressure. His world was never like this. It was always about either sex or money, somehow. Even his beloved poker games had an undercurrent of competition, and not just about the cards.

It seemed the most natural thing in the world to laugh too loud, to dance with abandon, to drink way more than was wise. One thing was for damn sure, he was in no condition to drive home.

"You okay?"

Gwen looked nice with her dark blond hair all loose around her shoulders. Or maybe it was the sheen. She looked sparkly, like her dress. "I need to find out if I can still get a room."

She seemed startled until she checked the slim silver watch on her wrist. "Wow. It's late. I mean early."

"Yeah."

"I hope they have two."

He nodded as exhaustion slammed him in the back of the head. "If not, we'll just get a taxi."

"Where do you live?"

"Los Feliz."

"That's pretty far."

"I know.

She looked up at him again. "I'm pretty drunk."

"I know that, too." Holding her hand, he led her out of the ballroom, all the way to the front desk. There were a few partygoers ahead of them, but that's not what made his step slow.

He looked at Gwen, at her pretty dress, at her pretty glow. The feel of her was still in his hands, in the rest of him. "Hey." He pulled her to a stop, then swung her around to face him. "How's about we only ask for one room."

"Why?"

He laughed. "You really have had a lot to drink if you have to ask."

She stared up at him as if he was out of his mind. And who knows. Maybe he was.

3

GWEN HADN'T BEEN THIS DRUNK since she'd stolen a bottle of blackberry schnapps from her parents' liquor cabinet in junior high. She felt as if she were still dancing, twirling into oblivion even as she stared up into dazzling dark brown eyes.

She knew she hadn't misheard or misread what he'd said. He wanted to finish the night off with a quickie. After a deep breath she got as steady as possible. "Are you insane? There's no way in hell I'm going to sleep with you."

His smile fell and he looked comically, drunkenly, disappointed. "Why not?"

Gwen pursed her lips, wishing both she and the room would stop spinning. "I'm drunk. Not stupid."

"Hey. I never said—"

"Come on." She tugged him closer to the front desk person. There were three people ahead of them. "Let's get our rooms, then sleep it off. You'll feel better in the morning."

"I don't see why you won't at least consider it."

The funny thing was, he didn't sound particularly smashed, but she knew how much he'd put away. Of course, the proof was in his offer. No way he would have wanted her if he was in his right mind. And frankly, although he was a fabulous dancer, he was involved with Autumn. That alone disqualified him. The thought made her shiver.

"Hey," he said again, only this time the single word was filled with a world of hurt.

"What?"

"I saw that cough-syrup look. I didn't think I was that bad."

Damn. She smiled as brightly as she could while trying to keep her balance. Oh, man, did her feet hurt. "That wasn't about you."

"Then what?"

"Autumn." She winced as soon as the word came out. She hadn't meant to say that.

"My Autumn?"

"Look. We're next."

He turned, overbalanced, but caught himself at the last minute. "I guess I drank a lot more than I thought. When we were dancing I didn't feel nearly this shaky."

She nodded, but stopped immediately as the motion made her stomach chime into a chorus of unsteadiness. The whole situation was ridiculous. She didn't want to stay at the hotel. She had nothing with her, no change of clothes, not even a toothbrush. But she also didn't want to take a taxi home, because just thinking of the ride made her queasy. Queasier.

At the front desk, it took Paul a few minutes to get out his wallet, then he slapped down a credit card. "Two rooms, please."

"I'm sorry, sir. All we have available is a single room."

"Two single rooms, then."

"Actually, there's only the one."

Paul looked at her. Then back at the reservation clerk. "We'll take it."

"Wait a minute." She drew Paul back a bit from the desk.

"Don't worry," he said, before she had a chance to protest. "You can have the room. I'll get a car."

"No. I'll get a car."

He shook his head. "Absolutely not. You need to go to bed."

"So do you."

He stared at her until he started swaying. "Fine. We'll share."

"Uh…"

"Don't worry. I'll be a perfect…uh…"

"Gentleman?"

He pointed at her. "Yes."

"Okay, then," she said.

Gwen wasn't worried—not about Paul, at least. She was concerned about not being ill. And the lack of a toothbrush. Along with the key, the nice reservation man handed Paul two baskets, each filled with all kinds of necessities. Everything they'd need to get through the night. Including two shiny condom packets.

As if.

THE ROOM WAS SERVICEABLE, the bed a queen. Gwen thought again about calling for a cab, but the night's excesses won. She took her little basket into the bathroom and closed the door.

The contents were enough to get her by, only just. No makeup remover, no face cream. She brushed her teeth as she debated the pros and cons of keeping her dress on. It was a beautiful thing and she wasn't sure how it would do if slept in. The alternative, however, was bra and panties. Perhaps if the lights were off. If he were asleep. If she could manage to remove her clothes without falling flat on her ass. As it was, she was barely keeping her balance with a hand on the counter.

She brushed her hair, then washed her face. It took a good deal of careful wiping to get most of her mascara off her eyes. When she was done she felt better. Slightly.

What she really needed was water. Lots of water.

When she came out, Paul was leaning against the wall, his tie off, his shirt half unbuttoned and his jacket on one of the chairs. Despite everything, he managed to look obscenely handsome. "It's all yours."

He gave her a decent smile, considering, and took her place behind the closed door. If she was going to take off her dress, now would be the time to do it. First, though, she got a bottle of water from the minibar, then she kicked off her shoes. As she yanked the covers down, the reality of sleeping in her dress seemed too uncomfortable. Before she could change her mind her dress was off and she was scrambling under the covers as quickly as her poor body would move.

The minute her head touched the pillow the seriousness of her folly hit hard. It had been years since she'd felt this horrible spinning sensation, years since she'd been fool enough to even approach being drunk.

Why? Why had tonight been so different? It wasn't just the pity date. She'd had plenty before and never gone overboard. It wasn't just her family and their stupid comments. If she wasn't used to that by now, she might as well just give up. It couldn't have been Paul. Yes, yes, gorgeous, right. But so what? She wasn't the one who was fixated on good looks. Or charm, for that matter.

None of her relationships, other than familial, were based on appearances. The only things she cared about were on the inside. She'd learned early that kindness was a huge thing, even more important than intelligence and wit. She'd built her life around that very principle, and it had made her, for the most part, happy.

Although Paul had shown kindness tonight, she wasn't at all convinced it was genuine. He was after Autumn. That revealed a great deal.

It didn't matter, in the end. She'd gotten drunk. So what. Tomorrow, her real life would continue. She'd remember the dancing which had been such a fun surprise. And she'd use tonight as another reminder that too much alcohol was not her friend.

For now, she'd be very happy if the damn room would stop whirling.

She heard Paul leave the bathroom, but she didn't turn to look at him. She closed her eyes, even though that made things a lot worse.

She felt the covers move, his weight dipping the mattress. The room went dark with the click of a switch. Then she felt him slide in beside her.

Her eyes open once again, she willed herself to pass out so she wouldn't be so very aware of this man, this virtual stranger, stretched out beside her. He groaned, and she sympathized. A few seconds later, after he'd made some adjustments, he stilled. She relaxed.

She could smell him.

Nothing at all unpleasant about it. Soap, clean skin. Damp hair. *Intimate.*

She became achingly aware that she was in her underwear. Her plain department store panties and bra.

Was he in his? Boxers? Briefs? Those sexy European trunks that looked so appealing in the magazines? Surely he wasn't naked.

Her eyes closed again, and this time, she was the one to moan. Not just from the dizziness, either.

"You okay?" he whispered.

"No. I'm an idiot."

He sighed. "Me, too. I can't stop spinning."

"I'm too old for this kind of nonsense." She shifted a bit on the bed, then froze, not wanting to touch him by accident. "Even when I was young I was too old for this."

"It's not all that dire. I, for one, will look back on this night not for being drunk off my ass, but for having a hell of a good time. I can't remember the last time I danced like that."

Gwen couldn't help her smile. "Yeah. It was pretty great."

She waited for him to speak again, but there was only the sound of his breathing. Perhaps he'd fallen asleep. Of course he had. It was absurdly late.

Once more, she closed her eyes and once more she

moaned. It was cut short by the touch of his hand on her arm. Under the covers.

"I can call down for some Alka-Seltzer," he said. "There wasn't any in the care baskets."

Should she move? No. She should ignore it. Him. "No, that's okay. The spinning will stop soon."

"Promise?"

"Wish I could."

"You know," he said, "it kind of helps to talk. At least for me. But that's nuts, so never mind."

"No, it's not," she said as she prayed he'd move his hand. "It does help, I think."

"Crap."

"What's wrong?" She almost turned. Didn't.

"I forgot to get water. Be back in a sec."

His hand lifted and she breathed again. As the bed jiggled it occurred to her that drunkenness wasn't her worst sin of the night. Being ridiculous had that honor. She was behaving like a child. A ninny. Like one of her sisters.

The light from the small fridge made her look. Boxers. Nice ones, though not the kind she'd been hoping for.

"You want one?" he asked.

"I'm good."

He stood there, bare but for his undies, his head back, water bottle at his lips. He drank greedily, and even in the weird light she could see his Adam's apple bob.

Okay, so she wasn't being a complete moron. The guy was outside of her experience. The situation was incredibly intimate. Who wouldn't feel intimidated?

Paul turned to face her, backlit to perfection. "That made all the difference. Are you sure you don't want one?"

"I've got a bottle right here." She tried to keep her gaze on his face, but her eyes refused to obey. They swept down his chest to his slim hips and below where they lingered until he closed the minifridge door.

He got back into bed with no hesitation this time. While she was busy worrying about the slightest touch, he not only made a good deal of noise, he moved until he was right next to her. If she rolled over, she'd be half on top of him.

"Would it be easier for you if I slept in the bathtub?" she asked.

"What? Why?"

She would have given him a withering glare, but it was dark and she was on her side facing away. "You seem to need a lot of room."

"No, actually, I don't. I just wanted to be close."

"I haven't changed my mind, Paul. Besides, you're in no condition."

"You're wrong about that, but I'm very clear that you said no. I won't press the issue."

"So what's with the close?"

"You smell nice. And I want to talk."

She swallowed at the compliment, then let it go for what it was. "Talk about what?"

"We can start with your famous bar buddies."

Gwen sighed. "Well then, move over."

He did, then she sat up, holding the covers over her chest as she put her pillow behind her back.

Paul evidently thought that was a good move, and he followed suit. "Bar buddies?"

"It's nothing. I go to a sports bar on Monday nights. They play sports trivia."

"Are you good?" he asked.

"I'm great."

Paul grunted.

"What?"

"Nothing."

She looked at him, more awake than she'd been a minute ago. "I won last year's overall championship."

"All sports?"

"All the major sports. It's not just a local contest, either. It's all over America and Canada. I happen to play at Bats and Balls, but there are hundreds of bars that participate."

"Whoa. Okay, sorry I questioned your expertise, but it still doesn't answer my question."

"Which was…?"

"Bar *buddies*."

"Men play there, too. Eve finds it suspicious that I hang out with men and we're all just friends."

He turned his head, although she couldn't make out his expression. "Eve's an idiot."

"Yes. She is," she said, quite definitely. Then she smiled, just because.

PAUL STRETCHED HIS NECK as he hunkered down in the bed. The dizziness, thank God, had eased and sleep was creeping up the blankets. Still, he didn't want Gwen to stop talking. He wanted to fade out on her soft voice. He wished that was all he wanted.

They'd talked baseball, moved on to football then somehow got onto favorite pizza joints, but he wasn't sure where she was now. He'd tuned out the words a while ago, concentrating on the sound. His thoughts had drifted as he'd been lulled by her low seductive tone. He knew he wouldn't be able to stay awake for more than a few minutes and dammit, he wanted to touch her. Just touch her.

She stopped talking and the quiet wasn't half as nice, but then she shifted until they were lying side by side with a more than decent space between them.

Paul turned to face her. When she didn't object, he inched a little closer. With the room so dark, he had no signals to tell him if she was cringing or amenable. The last thing he wanted was to freak her out. "You awake?" he whispered.

"Barely."

"Would you hate it if I got closer?"

She was silent for several seconds, which gave him all the answer he needed.

"Never mind. Sweet dreams." He closed his eyes, letting it go. It had been a foolish thought. He wasn't a cuddler, never had been. He was pretty damn sure this weird feeling had more to do with alcohol than desire.

That feeling came over him—a twilight kind of buzz that precedes slumber. He welcomed the sensation.

When she shifted again he didn't think anything of it. Not until her backside brushed his hip.

The buzz now in his body was of an entirely different nature. Oddly, he didn't go into sex mode. It wasn't about that. When he put his arm around her tummy, the softness of her skin felt perfect. When he spooned her so that he felt her body against his chest, his thighs, he smiled with contentment.

This was exactly what he'd wanted. And from her sigh, he knew she wasn't unhappy about it, either.

He closed his eyes and drifted off.

GWEN WASN'T SURE how long she'd been in his arms. All she knew was that Paul had fallen asleep, his body cupping hers in an embrace that should have had her running for a cab. Only she didn't want to run.

She couldn't remember the last time she'd felt so good. Even the headache that was just starting to bloom in her temples didn't bother her.

Maybe all of it—the way she'd danced like a fool, agreeing to spend the night, *this*—had a simple explanation. Touch.

She hadn't been touched in a long, long time. Maybe a handshake or two, but his palm on her tummy, her body pressed to his, that hadn't happened for what, six months? Longer?

No wonder she'd had difficulty saying no. People were wired to need contact. The more, the better. A huge part of pair bonding had to do with the chemicals humans released when they were skin to skin.

Not that she wanted to pair bond with Paul. Not only was his taste in women completely suspect, but he was just too good-looking.

No, except for his love of baseball…and poker, and dancing. And okay, he had a pretty good sense of humor and he liked horror flicks, still, there was nothing about Paul that appealed to her.

It was the touch thing. He hadn't been in Autumn's pants yet, so he'd been without for a while. One would assume. And Gwen hadn't been close to anyone since Alex. So she should just go to sleep now. Take comfort where it was offered and let the rest fade away.

She found his hand, the one draping her waist, and she put her own hand over his. She moved her leg and her back until she was perfectly comfy with maximum touching. She matched her breathing to his slow, even rhythm. Yet sleep didn't come.

Her weary, stupefied mind kept dancing. Not just to the swing band from earlier, but to the look of indignation on his face when Faith and Eve had said their horrible things. To the way his eyes had lit up when she'd confessed her Dodger addiction. To the way he moaned, just then, as he dreamed. As he held her.

As far as pity dates went, this one had been the best yet. A grand slam.

She yawned once, squeezed his hand, and that was it.

4

SHE WOKE TO THE NUDGE of a penis on her ass. Instantly alert, Gwen froze as panic swelled in her chest and made her Kong-sized headache pound. He had to be asleep. If he wasn't, then she was going to make damn sure he wouldn't be able to poke anyone again for a long, long time.

His hand was still around her waist, loosely, and his knees were neatly tucked behind hers. Warm breath hit the back of her neck and as she planned her escape, she relaxed a bit. He had to be sleeping.

Okay. So she couldn't be angry about his condition. She still needed to get up, grab her dress and make it to the bathroom without waking him.

Despite the darkness of the room she knew it was daylight. Parched and achy, all she wanted was to skip this part and be home. Instead, she held her breath as she carefully lifted his hand. Inch by inch she moved toward the edge of the bed, wincing in her effort not to screw up. She should never have stayed last night. What had she been thinking?

Almost…almost…

Her body was clear. She held on to his hand as she

pulled her pillow down to take her place. Hardly daring to breathe she sat up, turned to look at him.

Mistake.

He was as gorgeous as a movie-star hero. She had no illusions about what she looked like when she first got up. Life just wasn't fair, that's all. Anyway, his breathing hadn't changed, his eyes were closed and she'd better get her butt in gear if she intended to make a getaway.

Rising slowly, she made it to her feet. First, she grabbed the water bottle from the nightstand, then hurried to get her dress and dashed into the bathroom.

Finally, she could catch her breath. The woman in the mirror looked like hell, but at least she had a toothbrush and soap.

It didn't take her long to get dressed. The only thing missing from the bathroom was a notepad. It seemed really impolite to leave without some kind of goodbye. On the other hand, she'd never see Paul Bennet again, so why bother?

No, even she couldn't be that dismissive. He'd been nice. The best pity date ever. One she'd actually look back on fondly. With brush in hand, she opened the bathroom door to go hunt for paper.

Only Paul wasn't sleeping anymore. He stood directly in front of her, not five inches away. In his boxers. In the light. Looking like a god. He seemed a bit desperate as he moved quickly into the bathroom. She shook herself out of her beauty-induced shock and scurried out.

With her heart rate up and a ferocious desire to get the hell out of there, she turned on the light by the nightstand. A convenient Marriott notepad and pen were at the ready and she dashed off a quick thanks, tore that sheet off, then wrote another, this one nicer. Her purse was in her hand and she was halfway to the door when Paul came out of the bathroom.

She shouldn't have written that second note. It had given him time to wash his face, run a damp hand through his hair. She could also see that his poker was behaving once more. Why not? It wasn't as if he'd been hard over her.

"You taking off?"

"I need coffee and a shower."

"I hear that. I'm happy to call down for room service. I can be dressed in no time."

"It's okay. Stay." She forced herself to look at his face and only his face. "Take your time. I'm not that far, and I'll have no trouble getting a cab from here."

He nodded. "I understand."

If she wasn't mistaken, he sounded a little pouty, which didn't make sense at all. It was probably nothing. His head had to feel as badly as her own. She couldn't imagine him wanting to stretch things out.

"I wrote you a note. Now that you're here I'll just say thank you. I really did have a fun night. You're a hell of a dancer."

"Yeah. I had a good time, too. Weird, huh?"

"Very." She went to pass him, then he touched her arm.

"Autumn was right."

"About?"

"You being interesting and fun."

"I was drunk as a skunk, although I'm not really sure what that means."

His smile was slow and devilish. "Yeah, I think skunks are entirely too clever to drink as much as we did."

"Hangover?"

He nodded.

"I bet they have plenty of aspirin in the lobby. Anyway…"

"Yeah. Anyway…"

She looked down at where his hand touched her bare skin. Odd. The touch meant nothing. Completely innocent. Only it didn't feel that way.

A second later, she realized he was leaning toward her. She looked up just as his lips met her own.

Paul kissed her.

Again she froze, lips together, not breathing, waiting for something to happen. Him to back up with a start or a laugh or to ease his grip on her arm. What happened instead was that he continued to kiss her, tilting his head a bit to the right. Parting his lips.

Her eyes closed of their own volition, even as she told herself to move away, to stop the nonsense and get home where crazy things like sleeping with strangers didn't happen. What she did instead was part her lips, too.

Paul sighed and she inhaled his peppermint breath. Time stretched and slowed her thoughts and her reactions until she barely recognized herself.

As if poked with a stick, Paul jerked back, snatched his hand away. He looked completely startled. "Whoa. Sorry about that. I didn't mean—"

"No problem. Mistakes all around. Anyway…"

"Yeah, yeah." He backed up a step, then two. "Anyway…"

"I'll just be—"

"Sure. Good."

She flung out her hand, searching for the door. "It was fun. The dancing."

"Fun. Yes." He backed up until he hit the bed.

Luckily, she found the door and before she could utter another inane word, she was out in the hall. She leaned back, hitting her head pretty hard, swore soundly, then made her way to the elevator, wondering what in the hell had happened to her. It was all too strange, every bit of it, and she felt sure that if her head didn't hurt quite so much, she'd be able to make sense of the butterflies in her tummy. Or why the memory of his lips persisted. Why she felt the need to rub her arm where he'd touched her. Instead, she decided to pretend last night and this morning had never happened.

PAUL CHECKED his watch again. Autumn was later than usual for their dinner, and he was starving. He'd gotten their table at Nobu forty minutes ago, and the waiter was getting itchy. Paul had nursed his drink down to ice. Where was she? It had been her idea to come here, a thank-you for taking Gwen to the anniversary party. It had taken two weeks for her to come up with this dinner, changing plans at the last minute so they would meet here instead of him picking her up.

He really wasn't sure why he bothered. Autumn was hot, but forty-minutes-late hot? Two weeks of cajoling and teasing hot?

It had taken him a full twenty-four hours to recover from the evening with Gwen, and a lot longer than it should have to stop thinking about it. He could hardly believe that he'd wanted to sleep with Autumn's sister. Not only was she not at all his type, but the idea that he'd even considered doing something so unsavory made him wary of ever drinking again.

He knew a lot of guys, some of them good friends, who wouldn't think twice about going after a sister. He wasn't one of them. He liked to think he had standards. Okay, not terribly high standards, but he tried to adhere to simple rules. He never lied to any of his women about dating others. He didn't cheat when he'd made any kind of commitment. There simply wasn't a reason to.

He'd worried, right after, that Gwen would have told Autumn that he'd been stupid. The more he thought about it, the more he concluded she never would. She and Autumn weren't close, plus, Gwen had been appalled when he'd suggested sex.

And that had been gnawing at him.

She hadn't even given it a minute's thought. Her answer had been immediate and fervent. He hadn't had an outright rejection like that since he'd tried to get into Nina Jackson's pants after she'd told him she was saving herself for marriage. But he'd been in college back then and he'd had the moral fortitude of a garden snake.

Gwen, on the other hand, wasn't a child. He doubted she got a lot of invitations, so why had she reacted so strongly? The only thing he'd come up with was that she knew he was dating Autumn. That made sense.

He sipped the remnants of his drink as he looked around the restaurant. Everyone inside was young and attractive. Nobu was an L.A. hotspot. Celebrities showed up on a regular basis, there was always a cadre of paparazzi outside, and the food cost a damn fortune, but that was part of the cachet. Hard to imagine Gwen with him here.

Not that she was ugly, because she wasn't. Hell, there were well-known actresses and singers who aced that category, but they had something that Gwen didn't. He'd seen it in his work often, in fact. There was a certain air about a person who fit into the limelight. A charisma.

Gwen, he knew, would consider all this so much bullshit. She wouldn't be impressed with the crowd or the chance that she might see someone famous. She would think it ridiculous to pay so much for the privilege of dining in an A-list restaurant, even if the food was superb.

He put his glass down. Gwen wouldn't be so much out of place here as she would make him feel foolish for wanting her here.

Something caught his attention at the front of the restaurant and he sighed with relief that it was Autumn. She made her typical entrance. Flashy, bold as brass. Her dress was red and tight and short enough to really show off her exceptional legs. Her blond hair flowed over her shoulders like silk and when she walked, it was with the confidence of a woman who understood her power.

He stood and waited for it. Her dazzling smile came at the perfect time. The moment of greatest impact. The woman was wasting her talent on airplanes. At the very least, she should be modeling, at the most, ruling a kingdom. He suspected she was holding out for the latter. She'd told him several times that she was going to be switching routes to the Middle East instead of Europe and that could only mean she was going for the top prize. Some potentate with hot and cold running billions.

"Paul." She said the word in that big-screen way. Soft, yet it carried to the cheap seats.

He leaned over and kissed her cheek before she sat. The smell of her was enough to end all critical thought. Damn.

She immediately ordered a special Nobu martini, and he ordered another of his. The second they were alone, she gave him a look that alerted all his testosterone to be at the ready. "Rumor has it, you and Gwen had quite a night."

"Are you still on that? I told you. We danced. It was fun. I was glad to do it."

"According to Faith, you weren't doing me any favors."

"What?"

"She said when you two got to the slow dances, a breeze couldn't have gotten between you."

"Gwen's a good dancer."

Autumn stared at him for a long moment, then burst into bright laughter. "Oh, my God. Your face! As if you and Gwen…" She laughed some more, garnering as much attention as she could without going a millimeter overboard. "She must have died when she saw you at her door. Oh, I wish I could have seen it."

"It wasn't all that funny."

"Come on, Paul. I know my sister. It must have been something." A delicate sniffle and a touch of her napkin at the outer corner of her eye, and then she looked at him once more. "I appreciate what you did. It had to have been awful for you. Faith said you acted like a real gentleman the whole night. She could barely believe you didn't sneak out at the first opportunity."

Paul picked up his menu, bothered more than he should have been at the way Autumn spoke about Gwen. Best to leave it alone. Autumn's relationship, if he could call it that, to her sister wasn't his business. But jeez. "I'm glad I could help. Did you want to start with appetizers?"

The moment Autumn picked up her menu he shifted gears. It wasn't wise to think about Gwen now. He wanted to get through dinner and get to the good part with Autumn. He'd bought new condoms for the occasion.

He watched her, amazed as always at her sheer beauty. She had a quality about her that was the essence of what he'd been thinking about before. Charisma, magic, that something extraordinary that made strangers ask for her autograph. He'd seen it happen often. Even after she explained she wasn't anyone noteworthy, they wanted her to sign the paper, the menu, their hand. She always did, too, as if it was the most natural request in the world.

Autumn lived out loud. She shimmered in the light. There was no way to ignore her.

Gwen kept her light inside. Private.

He couldn't imagine that the two of them were related. Maybe their mother had had that affair with the postman after all.

"I'll have the lobster ceviche and after that I'd like the toro tartar when he gets his main dish."

He hadn't realized the waiter was there until Autumn ordered so he made a quick decision and that was that.

Their drinks arrived a moment later and Autumn changed the subject to her adventures in Rome.

He listened, enchanted as always. She didn't require much from her audience so he didn't worry overmuch when his thoughts wandered to what the night promised. They'd go back to his place. His maid had been there that afternoon, so everything was just right. He had champagne in the fridge and some very expensive beluga.

"What are you thinking about?"

"Hmm? Oh. You. Of course. Only you."

GWEN POURED THE POPCORN from the popper and spread it on a cookie sheet. She got out the butter-flavored cooking spray and spritzed the whole pan, then covered the corn with her signature chili, lime and salt mix.

"Bring me a beer when you come?"

Gwen poured the popcorn into a giant bowl, grabbed Holly her beer and herself a diet soda, and headed back into the living room.

Holly was spread out on the couch like a contented cat. She'd worn her pajamas over, the ones with the cowboys on them, and her fuzzy slippers. When the movie was over, she'd go up two floors to her own apartment. It was perfect. Especially because Holly also worked at Rockland-Stewart, where they'd met. They'd hit it off immediately and when the apartment upstairs had become vacant, Holly had jumped all over it.

"Are we ready?" Gwen asked. "Is there anything else we're missing?"

Holly took her beer, popped the top and grabbed a handful of popcorn as Gwen sat down. "Nope. I think everything is perfect. Except that we're here, in our jammies, watching movies on a Friday night."

"In my opinion that is the essence of perfection." She opened her soda and poured it into her big glass.

Holly pointed the remote at the DVD player, but she didn't press the button. "I think Ito likes you."

"What?"

"I think he's crushin' on you something fierce."

Gwen couldn't help but laugh. "Ito? You're totally high. I'm his competition. He hates that my numbers are larger than his."

"Nope. He's hot for you. He wants you."

"Press the button, Holly."

"Yes, ma'am." She pressed it and the FBI warning came on, then she pressed the button again. "Oh my God, I can't believe I forgot to tell you. I saw a picture of Paul Bennet. Why didn't you tell me he's more gorgeous than Brad Pitt?"

"Because he isn't. Can we see the movie now?"

Holly gave her a withering look. "How can we possibly be friends when you're this obnoxious."

"Thank you. Let me wipe a tear at that lovely compliment."

"Shut up. He was maybe the best-looking man I've ever seen. I don't know what I would have done if I'd opened my door to that."

"He's dating Autumn."

"So he's not bright. Exceptions can be made."

"No," Gwen said sharply. "They can't."

"What was it like to be in his arms?" Holly asked, as if Gwen hadn't objected.

"He was a good dancer. Once I was drunk, easy to talk to."

Holly took a handful of popcorn. "He likes the Dodgers." Then she popped each piece into her mouth, one at a time.

"We're in L.A. It's not a big shock."

"He got you a room. That was nice."

"Charming. Let's move on." She winced at how bitchy she sounded, but she didn't want to answer any more questions about that night. She barely wanted to think about it, although she hadn't had much luck there.

"Why are you doing this to me?" Holly gave her a mighty pout. "I have nothing going on in my love life. I need more than online gossip and office politics. He's the most interesting thing that's happened to us in ages."

"He's dating Autumn. I haven't given him a thought since that night." Lightning didn't strike at the lie. "Now can we please watch Mr. Willis kick some end-of-the-world ass?"

"You're no fun."

Gwen stuffed popcorn in her mouth. Pissed once again at her inability to erase everything to do with Paul Bennet from her memory. Damn him.

PAUL GOT THE CHAMPAGNE out of the fridge and popped the cork. He brought the bottle up to his mouth to catch the overflow, not giving a damn when most of it hit the floor.

He grabbed the tin of caviar and a spoon, and sat down at the bar in his kitchen. Alone.

She'd done it to him again. He'd been hopeful to the last second. The valet had taken his tip, Autumn had stood at the door of her Lexus, and he'd opened his mouth to tell her to follow him when she'd delivered the death blow. As much as she'd love to join him in an intimate night of sin, it couldn't happen tonight. Girl trouble.

She'd actually said, "Girl trouble." He'd seen from the look on her face that she thought she was being adorable.

He'd explained that he was a big boy and didn't care about girl trouble, but she wouldn't budge. She'd kissed him, as if that would make everything just fine, and she'd driven off, leaving him with a hard-on and a renewed determination that it was over. It was bullshit. He didn't need her kind of crap, even if she turned out to be the best lay in the Western world.

He took a spoonful of caviar then lifted the bottle for a champagne chaser.

Screw her. She could play her games all she wanted. He was out of there.

He pulled out his cell phone and hit speed dial seven. Laurie never had girl trouble. And she had always been amenable to the booty call.

She answered. Two minutes later he put the cork back in the bottle, the top back on the caviar, and he was on his way.

5

THE SCORE WAS FIVE TO FOUR in the ninth and Takashi Saito was on the mound. It was three and two, and this pitch would make or break the game. Not one of the eight people at Gwen's table said a word. In fact, she doubted anyone was breathing as Saito leaned in for the pitch.

The batter swung. Missed it by a mile and the whole bar roared with victory. The Dodgers had won and in this bar, that meant spilled beers and high fives all around.

Gwen whooped it up with the best of them. The season was shaping up nicely for her boys, and she couldn't be happier. It had been too long since the Dodgers had been in the winners circle. She had great hopes that they'd take it all the way this year.

Holly, who wasn't much of a sports freak, celebrated anyway, glad to be out with friends at Bats and Balls. The gang consisted of folks from work plus a few extra mates or dates, enough of them to fill up their long picnic table.

There would be a ten-minute break before the trivia started. Six members of her group were die-hard players. As a team they were nearly always in the top ten. Individually, no one came close to her record.

Yes, it was compulsive, her love of stats and game

minutiae, but screw it. Baseball gave her pleasure. Watching it, talking about it, and even playing it. Rockland-Stewart had a team that played against other employment firms. She managed The Rocks and played third base. They were okay, had even won the championship three years ago, though it was mostly for the fun and the after-game pizza.

All in all, this was her favorite night of the week. The whole group took it seriously, and no matter what was going on at work they all bonded over America's pastime.

Holly nudged her in the arm and held up her empty beer glass. "You want another?"

Gwen shook her head at the waitress standing just behind her. "Club soda, please." She hadn't had much more than that in the two weeks since her parents' party. She'd never gone overboard when it came to liquor, and that night had reminded her why.

"Did you win?"

Gwen hadn't thought about the weekly pool since she'd given Ken her money. "Nope. I never do."

"Me, neither." Holly leaned closer. "What do you think of Ellen's date?"

Ellen was one of the accounting staff. She was in her twenties, pretty, in good shape. She wasn't a great baseball fan, but she did love picking up guys at the bar. Gwen didn't recognize this one. She'd probably met him elsewhere. He was just the kind of man Ellen liked—buff, tall, handsome, if one went for that type.

Ellen laughed at something her current beau said, but stopped short. Her wide-eyed gaze fixed on someone at the front door.

Beside Gwen, Holly whispered, "Holy shit."

Gwen knew just what she meant. A shiver raced up her spine as she saw none other than Paul Bennet. No tuxedo this time. Just jeans and a pale blue work shirt; the man could stop traffic. Did stop traffic. Every woman in the bar had gone silent.

Gwen could feel her cheeks heat with a blush that made her furious. What was he doing here? Was he with Autumn? That would ruin everything. Dammit, this was her bar, her friends. This was where she came to forget about the real world, including her foolish family.

Paul caught her eye and he smiled.

"Oh, my heaven, he's coming over here." Holly fluffed her curly hair and licked her lips. Gwen didn't look, but she would bet good money that Ellen was doing the same thing. Had he come here looking for her? For God's sake, why?

He walked to the table, right up to her. "Hey. You have room for one more?"

Gwen looked up at him. Despite her obvious displeasure at his intrusion her body reacted without her consent. All manner of butterflies and heart pounding. "What are you doing here?"

His smile held up, despite the rude question. "I had to see you in action. Am I too late for the trivia?"

"No." Holly pushed her chair over, practically knocking Ken over in her haste. "It hasn't started yet. There's a chair right behind you. I'll get you a machine."

Paul didn't waste a moment. He didn't have to. Holly stole the chair from behind them and blushed like a teenager when he offered her a soft "Thanks." By the time he sat down, she was back with his game player, the electronic gadget that connected this bar and all the others to the national scoreboard.

"What, no Autumn?" Gwen asked.

Paul shook his head. "No, I'm here all by myself. Couldn't help wondering if you were really as good as you claimed to be."

Smart-ass. "I guess we'll see."

He leaned closer, and even though the room smelled of beer and hot wings and too many men who were vague about the whole bathing concept, his scent came to her, that clean, intimate smell she remembered. She didn't want to smell his neck, or any other part of him.

"I honestly hope you don't mind. If it's a problem, I'm out of here."

"Why would I mind? It's a public place."

He looked at her with knowing eyes and, if she wasn't mistaken, a hint of hurt. "I'm overwhelmed at your welcome. Listen, I'll go. It's not a big deal."

She put her hand on his arm as he started to stand. "No, don't be silly. I was just surprised to see you, that's all. You don't even live in this neck of the woods."

"You mentioned the place when we were at the party. There aren't many sports bars called Bats and Balls in Pasadena."

"That's true. And you are welcome. The waitress should be here in a second. They make great wings, if you haven't eaten."

"I'm good, thanks."

"You know how to play this game?"

"I've played trivia." He looked at the scorekeeper. All

the questions were multiple choice, broadcast on big screens throughout the joint. There were only five buttons for the play, but there was a keypad to log in.

"You need to pick a nickname," Holly said, leaning so far over the table she was almost in his lap.

"Oh?"

Still flustered, Gwen realized she'd made no introductions. And that everyone at the table was staring at her as if she'd grown a third eye. "Holly Quentin, this is Paul Bennet."

"Hi." Holly stuck out her hand, not even noticing that Paul had to shift halfway around in his chair to reach her.

"Everyone, this is Paul Bennet." Besides the noise of the joint, Gwen wanted questions kept at a minimum, so she made the intro generic. "Paul, this is everyone."

He nodded a general hello. That wasn't enough for the women at the table. First up was Ellen. Then Gina, Steph and Tara. They all gave him first and last names, how they knew Gwen and what they did at the office.

If she'd been alone, Gwen would have buried her head in her hands. My God, did this happen to him everywhere? Every day? It must be exhausting.

"Thank you all for letting me crash this party." He turned to Gwen, "What's this about a nickname?"

"Turn the thing on. It'll ask for a log-in. Use anything you like that's not obscene or too long."

"Damn."

"What?"

He looked at her with a perfectly straight face. "My buddies call me Bodhisattva, but I guess that would be too many letters, huh?"

Even she had to smile at that one. "I'll just bet they do."

"I'm a very spiritual person."

"Uh-huh."

"Every time Furcal comes to bat, I pray for a triple."

"No wonder we haven't been in the World Series for years."

The waitress came with the drinks, and Paul raised an eyebrow at Gwen's club soda. He ordered a Heineken then he typed in his nickname and pressed the button. The name appeared on the master board. Newbie.

"All right, Newbie," she said. "Prepare to be served."

"Care to make it interesting?"

He'd leaned into her space again. His shoulder touched her shoulder. She actually wanted things to be less interesting. It made no sense that he was here. Baseball trivia was a swell game, but come on. He stuck out like an incredibly good-looking thumb. Not just because of his looks, either. He had an aura about him. As if he were somehow still wearing the tux, and that he'd have a limo outside, waiting, complete with supermodel and champagne chilling. He most certainly didn't belong with her. "How interesting?"

She wasn't about to let him know that he was giving her fits. In fact, she didn't dare look around. She knew what she'd see. All of her coworkers would now be staring at her with giant question marks in their eyes. What was a man like him doing with a woman like her?

Even if Paul had come for the reason he'd stated, it wasn't okay. She didn't want to be buddies or pals or whatever the hell he thought they could be. The other night had been pleasant in spite of the reaction of her family to their pairing. She'd put up with the insults because she'd known there was an end in sight.

That's what got her, of course. That everyone thought it so unbelievable that she could possibly attract a man like him. It shouldn't upset her because it was true. She couldn't. Not in this world, in this lifetime. Yet she didn't appreciate everyone else acting as if they were the most improbable twosome since Quasimodo hit on Esmeralda.

"You win," he said, reminding her he'd wanted to wager on the outcome, "I take you to my box at Dodger Stadium."

"I have season tickets," she said.

"Oh. In a luxury suite?"

That made her turn in her chair. "No, you do not."

"Ah, but I do."

"For the whole season?"

"The whole season."

How was she supposed to turn that down? She'd never been inside one of the suites, but she'd heard all about them. The view was awesome, there were seven TV monitors including a forty-five-inch liquid crystal flat panel. A private concourse and lounge. It was all catered, even if all you wanted were Dodger Dogs and popcorn. There was even concierge service. Shoes could be shined while one sipped friggin' champagne. There was no choice. "You're on."

"Hey, wait a minute," he said. "What do I get if I win?"

"You won't."

For the first time since they'd met, he looked shocked. "Cocky, are we? You have no idea how much I know about baseball."

"I've beat the whole country at this game."

"You haven't played me."

"True. So what do you want on the incredibly, infinitesimally slim chance that you win?"

"I have to think about it."

"Don't think too long. The game's about to start."

Little clicking sounds of machines being turned on filled the room. Laughter came from one side, a murmur of excitement from another. Gwen figured it was safe to look around, finally, but she was wrong.

Her teammates, at least the females, ignoring their machines and the big screens, were focused on Paul. She cursed under her breath and fixed her gaze on the screen.

The big introduction came first, followed by a quick recap of the rules. Then, the questions began, easy at first, but pretty soon they'd start to get tough. Then really tough. Ending with brutal.

"Okay." His voice startled her being so near to her ear. "I win, I take you to a game in my suite."

She turned to stare at him. He was so close if she'd leaned over a couple of inches her lips and his would meet. Again.

She jerked back, her thoughts a jumble of nonsense and by the time she got a sliver of calm back, she'd missed the first question altogether.

"You're gonna have to do better than that," Paul said, his soft chuckle just this side of annoying.

She took a big swig of club soda, then settled her game pad. "Hold on to your shorts, big guy. I'm gonna whip you so hard you're gonna cry for your mama."

PAUL LAUGHED as the second question came up. *Which of the following played in 24 all-star games for the National League, and one for the American League?* He knew the answer even before the multiple choices appeared on the board. Hank Aaron, of course. If this was as hard as the questions got, he was going to kick ass. Not that it mattered all that much. He enjoyed winning, too much, most of the time, but his real purpose in participating wasn't the trivia.

He hadn't planned on inviting her to a game. Hell, he hadn't planned on ever seeing Gwen again. But he'd kept thinking about her.

Not the way he kept thinking about Autumn, even though he'd resolved to forget about her. No, his thoughts had turned to Gwen for a slew of other reasons. He'd really had a good time at the anniversary party. He'd liked the dancing, sure, but mostly he'd liked the fact that there had been no pressure. He hadn't been trying to score, not really. So the night had been just what it was.

She was interesting. Autumn hadn't lied about that. Smart, funny, and damn, she might be the first woman he'd ever known that liked sports as much as he did.

The next question came up, but he knew that answer, too. This was going to be a piece of cake.

He grinned at Gwen and she grinned back. She might not be the kind of woman he'd want in his bed, but to hang out with? Yeah, he could definitely see that. Not at his usual haunts, no, but he liked this bar. Liked the low-key atmosphere.

The only place he went these days where it was easy

was poker, and even that had too much pressure. He'd never done well solo, so he was always finding himself at clubs or at parties where the law of the jungle prevailed.

When was the last time, at least before the anniversary party, he'd felt relaxed? When every move hadn't been calculated to get him either a client or a woman?

It was time he had a friend. Admittedly it was odd that the friend in question was a woman. He'd never believed that it would be possible, but this might work.

"Gwen didn't tell me you were into baseball."

He turned to Holly, keeping half an eye on the big screen for the next question. "I'm a fool when it comes to baseball. And football. Basketball. Soccer, not so much."

"Boy, no wonder you two get along. She's the biggest sports nut I know."

"You two work together?"

Holly nodded. She was a reasonably attractive girl, even though she wasn't terribly polished. Her hair was a wild mass of blondish curls that didn't do a lot for her. Then there were the eyebrows. But her skin was good and her smile friendly.

Autumn would have dismissed her without a second glance, would accuse him of slumming. He saw it as expanding his repertoire. So what that none of these women would ever appear on the cover of a magazine. They were real. And he needed some real in his life.

"What about you?" He glanced at her Nomar Garciaparra T-shirt, the Dodger third baseman the women all seemed to love. "Is that just to fit in with the natives?"

"I love me some Nomar," she said, "but honestly I

come here for the people. I never even try to win at this—oh, another question."

He pressed the correct button, then noticed her hit one that was terribly wrong. No use butting in. She clearly didn't care if she lost.

Gwen, however, did. He wasn't keeping close enough track of her picks, but from her sly smile he gathered she was finding this as easy as he was. He wished the questions would get more challenging.

"One more, then there's a break," Holly said. "Round two is harder."

"So Gwen said. She's pretty good at this stuff, huh?"

"Amazing. I have no idea how she keeps all of it in her head. And it's not just sports. No one will play Trivial Pursuit with her anymore because she always wins. She's got one of those brains."

Paul nodded. "Thanks for the warning."

"Don't get me wrong. She's a really good sport about it. I mean she hardly ever gloats."

"Hardly ever?"

"Only if someone's being an asshole about winning. Men, I mean."

"We can be real jerks."

"I'm sure you're not."

He answered the final question of the round. "I wouldn't bet on it."

He felt Gwen's attention, even though he wasn't looking her way. Not sure how, but he absolutely knew she was listening. He kept his gaze on Holly. "Then she's not going to cry when I win this thing tonight?"

Holly smiled. "Uh, no."

"Not even in secret? Come on. You can tell me."

"Well, she did cry this one time—"

"Holly." Gwen's voice carried over all the room chatter. "What the hell are you telling him?"

"Nothing. I swear."

Paul checked his grin as he turned to Gwen. "It's okay. I understand. Women get all emotional, and that's part of their charm."

"I don't get all emo—" She stopped. Gave an enormous sigh. "You are an evil man. You tricked me with all the dancing, but now I see it. You're just evil."

"Me? Nah. I'm the sweetest guy you'll ever meet."

The look she gave him was actually unsettling. It wasn't at all what he was used to. The women he knew tended to have their own agendas blocking most honest interactions, and truth be known he wasn't any different. But Gwen—her eyes were clear, her evaluation of him held no slack.

If there was going to be a friendship with her, it would be on the level. Straight up, no bullshit. He hadn't had a friendship like that since high school. Huh. Tom Sutherland. They'd been close from the middle of grade school until just after high school graduation. He hadn't thought of Tom in a long time. He'd had a stare like Gwen's, only Tom's eyes weren't such a bold green. They weren't quite as unflinching. And, of course, he hadn't been a woman.

Gwen's expression changed as he watched, her examination of him growing more intense by the second. Finally, she asked a question that took him totally by surprise. "What's this about, Paul? Really?"

Honesty. No bullshit. He would stick to the game plan. "I hope we can be friends."

"Why?" she asked, too quickly. "I've already earned you all the points I can with Autumn. She won't think this is charming. In fact, it will make her think less of you."

He'd figured that out for himself, but he didn't want to talk about Autumn. "I enjoyed myself the other night, and I'm enjoying myself now. I have a feeling you're someone worth knowing."

Gwen's expression changed once more. This time he wished he hadn't seen it. Her look made it perfectly clear that she didn't share his desire for friendship. That, in fact, she didn't find him worth knowing at all.

He called the waitress back, not sure what to do. Crack a joke? Flirt with Holly? Ask Gwen to reconsider?

Reconsider? Why would *he* want to be with someone who didn't want *him?* He had no idea. The whole thing was preposterous. He wanted Autumn, not Gwen. Autumn, with her sexy laugh, her amazing curves and that stunningly beautiful face. Yeah, so why should he give a damn that her less-than-beautiful sister didn't want to be friends? He shouldn't. But he did.

6

IT WAS THE LAST ROUND of questions, those that separated the wannabes from the major leaguers. Gwen was two up from Paul, and while that pleased her, it wasn't quite as satisfying as it should have been, given she'd obviously hurt his feelings.

Tough.

She looked over at him, so artfully hiding that he'd been wounded by their exchange. What did he expect? He'd come uninvited. He was Autumn's bonbon and in different circumstances Paul and she would never have crossed paths. Now he wanted to be friends?

The question came up on the board. *Judge Kennesaw Mountain Landis was the first Commissioner of Baseball. Who was the seventh?* Damn. It had to be Giamatti. If not, well, she was still one up on Paul.

Giamatti, it was.

She glanced at Paul's machine, but couldn't tell if he'd gotten it right. He'd shifted his seat so he faced the table squarely instead of tilting a bit toward her.

Which brought her right back to feeling guilty.

This time when the waitress came around, Gwen eschewed her club soda and went for the beer.

If they hadn't been in the middle of a table full of coworkers, she'd have talked to him. Asked him again what had really prompted his trip. He didn't belong here, any more than she would belong at Fashion Week.

He'd certainly sounded sincere, but that's what he did for a living. Sadly, she wouldn't put it past her sister to have made this evening some kind of test or maybe even a dare.

Gwen had toyed with the idea of moving out of California. Rockland had other offices, including one in New York. She'd never lived anywhere but SoCal, still, being this close to her family simply wasn't good for her health. There were birthdays and anniversaries and weddings and all manner of holidays and she could only come up with so many excuses not to attend.

Next up her sister Bethany and husband, Harry, were having a big birthday bash for Gwen's niece, Nickie, who would turn one. Gwen had been roped into bringing her famous red velvet cupcakes, which meant she really couldn't bow out, even though she'd rather have a root canal.

There were only a few questions left, and Gwen put all her energy into answering them correctly. No distractions allowed. She aced the first one. Dammit, she missed the second. Got lucky on the third. The last one, though, was a gift. She'd just read the answer in one of her dozens of baseball books. She pressed the button and sat back in her chair. No gloating yet. Not until she saw how Paul did. The final scores always took about ten minutes, so she'd just relax and wait.

Holly appeared behind her and gave her a whack on her upper arm. "Come with me."

"Where?"

"Just come with me."

Gwen knew that tone. She excused herself to Paul and obediently trotted behind Holly to the ladies' room.

Holly folded her arms. Not a good sign. "What are you doing?"

"What are you talking about?"

"First, you completely lied about how gorgeous Paul is."

"Hey—"

"We can talk about that later. Now, I want to know why you're being such a bitch."

Gwen tried to keep her temper. "I realize it might be difficult to think of Paul as a person, but try, okay? I didn't invite him here. I hardly know him. Why should I bend over backward?"

"Bend over? Please. You're acting like he's got the plague."

"I am not."

Holly's eyes widened and she stepped closer to Gwen. This time, when she yelled, it was in a whisper. "I know when you're being nice and when you're not. You're not. Even if you don't like the guy, he hasn't done anything bad. So ease up. Give him a break."

"You're only saying this because he's handsome. Well, screw handsome."

Holly sighed. "I wish. But it's not true. I'm saying this because you're not that kind of person. Even when you're pissed off, you've got more class than anyone I know. Just, I don't know, ease up. He's a guest, invited or not. You don't have to talk to him ever again if you don't want to, but while he's at our table…"

"Yes, Mom. Do I have to wait for you, or can I go back and see the scoreboard?"

"You may go back."

Gwen touched her friend's arm. "I'll try."

The smile she received in return let her know that all was well. At least with Holly.

Was she truly being a bitch? She'd figured she was just being honest. But maybe the guilt didn't have to do with what she said so much as her overall attitude.

Paul stood as she came back to her funky chair at the beat-up old table. He sat only after her tush touched down. Yeah. He really fit in.

"When do we find out who won?" he asked, but his voice was tight, his expression unreadable.

"Any minute now." She turned her chair so she faced him. "What did you think of the questions?"

He took in a deep breath, then let it go. When he answered, it was Paul again. Completely confident and more than pleasant. "Easy, medium, hard. As warned. And the hard were really hard."

"That's a good thing?"

"Wouldn't be fun if it was all two plus two."

"My thoughts exactly."

Paul's shoulders relaxed. The smile he'd pasted on just a moment ago turned into something far more natural and pleasing. Maybe Holly had been right.

"Look, about this friendship thing…"

"Hey, I was rude—"

"No." Paul held up a hand to stop her. "I get it. Putting aside my exceptional dancing skills, I haven't given you much to admire. Even if I win tonight, it doesn't say anything real about me. And I know how you feel about Autumn, so…"

"Yeah. I haven't said many nice things about her, have I?"

"She's not all that bad, but I get your point. You two are night and day."

"Which has a lot to do with my, uh, curiosity about you showing up here. Did Autumn—"

"Autumn has no idea where I am. Or with whom I choose to spend my time."

"I see."

"I realize it was out of line for me to just show up here—"

"It wasn't. It's nice that you came."

He turned more toward her. "Really?"

"Confusing, but nice."

"Confusing, huh? Yeah, I guess I see your point. Anyway, what do you say? Will you come with me to the game? You pick the day."

Nothing about this made any sense. She couldn't quite get over the idea that Autumn had something to do with this, but man, she wanted to see a game from one of the suites. What was the worst that could happen? "Who else will be there?"

"No one. Unless you want to invite some of your friends."

"You want me to go with you to the game."

He nodded. "Does that sound so strange?"

Now it was her turn to nod.

"Do it anyway. You won't believe the view. Not to mention the food."

"Over first or third?"

He grinned. "First."

"Can I still get a dog?"

"All you want."

She sighed. "Okay. We'll give it a try."

He put his hand on hers and gave it a squeeze. "Excellent."

She almost backed out right then. Not because of his reaction, but because of her own. Her throat had tightened and her belly was doing stupid things, and why? Because he'd touched her. Absurd. With a smile that was as nice as she could make it, she slipped her hand from under his.

"This Sunday?" he asked.

"Sure. Sounds great."

"Is that the final score?" He was nodding toward the big screen behind her.

She looked at the names. Newbie was number one. She had come in second, by one point.

"Well, I'll be damned," he said, with just a bit of a gloat.

The others at the table weren't so gallant.

"Sonofabitch!" Ken actually got to his feet and held out his beer for a toast. "The queen has been knocked off her throne."

"No wonder you didn't want him here," Ellen said as she tapped her glass against Ken's.

"I knew we should have had side bets." Steph nodded toward Paul. "I could have made a fortune."

"Thanks, but it was only one point."

Ken made a rude sound. "Close only counts in horse-shoes, buddy. You kicked her ass. Not that we don't take a great deal of pride in our Gwen."

Holly slugged Ken in the arm. "You're only saying that because she's your boss."

"True."

Gwen had to smile. She knew they all meant well. She wasn't thrilled that she'd lost, but she did have to admit Paul hadn't lied about his knowledge of baseball. Maybe the day at the park would be fun. And maybe he was telling the truth about the rest.

Maybe.

PAUL FINISHED HIS PHONE CALL with Maggie Crawford at Imagine Films, then leaned back in his chair to stare out his window. It had been a brutal week. Lots of people not being where they were supposed to be. People not signing contracts. Lawyers and agents and all the other crap that were part and parcel of the business but the stuff he hated.

At least it was over, and Sunday the Dodgers were playing the Braves. Plus one.

He'd almost canceled about five times since Monday night. He had no business asking Gwen to come with him, and yet he'd never managed to make the call that would put an end to it.

No wonder Gwen had looked at him as if he were nuts. He was. He had friends. Plenty of them. All of them were guys, but so what? He'd never thought much about having a woman friend, and he wasn't convinced he could or should have one now.

Then what was this about? He didn't want to sleep with her. He had nothing to gain by her acquaintance. They both loved baseball, but again, so what?

He tried to come up with good reasons for not canceling. All he could manage was that it wouldn't be so bad.

As he relaxed, as his defenses went down, he remembered for the hundredth time the real reason for wanting to back out of this "date."

When she'd implied he wasn't someone worth knowing, it had hit him so hard he'd lost his bearings. Not for long, he was too good at his job for that, but shit, it had been rocky for a few seconds there. It had felt like a slap in the face. Like a gut punch. What had sent him reeling wasn't that he'd been insulted. It was because he'd had no comeback. Nothing. Zilch. Why *would* she want to know him?

He was flash. The sizzle, not the steak. He got away with most everything, always had. It was so easy with women he hardly had to try. In his business his face was his most important asset and he knew it. No sweat there.

He'd come up with a lot of reasons he should be worth knowing. He'd graduated from Yale. He knew all the celebrities that mattered. He had money. He could get into the best restaurants all over the world. He was Paul Bennet, and that had always mattered.

Only not with Gwen. Not one of the things on his list would impress her. Except for Yale, though somehow he knew she understood he hadn't gotten by on brains.

With Gwen, it was all about substance, and the truth was, he didn't have much. His charity work and donations were less about giving than getting. He made sure every donation was well publicized. He didn't have a belief system so much as a code that put him first, everyone else second. When had he last read a book that wasn't about sports or money? When had he had a conversation about anything that mattered?

And why the hell did he want to?

It was crazy. He was crazy. Had to be. There was nothing about his life that everyone he knew didn't envy. That was as it should be. He'd been born in the right place at the right time. Why shouldn't he enjoy it?

All his life he'd, well, underestimated people like Gwen. Those who didn't meet his standards. People who didn't matter to the tabloids had rarely mattered to him. It had been easier that way. It kept his world view controllable. Why mess that up now?

"Paul?"

He clicked on his intercom. "Yeah?"

"Someone's here to see you. She doesn't wish me to give her name. She wants it to be a surprise."

"Send her in."

He straightened up, ran a hand through his hair, wondering if it could be Gwen. He felt a little surge of anticipation as he stood.

The door opened and in walked Autumn. The small stab of disappointment knocked him back to his senses. Autumn was all soft hair, big eyes and long legs. They hadn't spoken since that night at Nobu, and for the life of him he couldn't recall why he'd thought that was a good idea.

"I owe you an apology," she said, moving toward him with a sway that would tempt a monk.

"For what?"

"For leaving you the other night. I was so naughty. And after all you did for me."

She'd reached his desk, and then she moved around it so she was just in front of his chair. She put her hands on the armrests and leaned over close enough for him to catch a whiff of the essence of sin.

He tore his gaze away from her face just so he could appreciate the view of her breasts. They were perfect. Her low-cut dress combined with the modern wonders of the push-up bra and he stopped castigating himself about past mistakes to concentrate on mistakes he could make right now.

"You probably have a date tonight, so I won't keep you." Even her breath made him hard.

"There is no one but you."

She smiled. "You always say the sweetest things."

"Give me five minutes to make sure Tina's gone. I'll lock the door."

That wasn't the right answer according to her tiny pout. "That sounds nice, but I was thinking…"

He doubted that, but went along with it anyway. "About?"

"There's a big party tonight at the Chateau Marmont. I thought we could go together. Just you and me."

"And a hundred of our closest friends?"

"It's going to be a really good party."

He sighed. Autumn was Autumn. Knowing her, she'd had another escort lined up, but something had happened, so she'd turned to Paul. And, knowing her, at the end of the evening, there would be a kiss or two, maybe a little more, but even though the party was at a hotel with beds and room service there would be no sex.

Gwen had told him how to woo Autumn, but he hadn't believed it. If he was smart, he'd send her on her way. Go home. Read a book. Watch something on PBS.

Autumn leaned down just far enough to run the tip of her tongue over his bottom lip.

After the shiver that went straight to his cock died down enough for him to breathe, he said, "Do you want dinner first?"

7

THERE WAS SOMETHING sinful about riding in a stretch limo wearing faded jeans and an old Dodgers T-shirt. Gwen should have met Paul at the stadium, but he'd insisted on picking her up. If she'd known it was going to be in this gas guzzler, she'd have flat out refused.

"Come on. It's not that bad. Some people would actually enjoy this little luxury."

Maybe she was being too harsh. He was trying very hard to win her over, and for Paul, a limo equaled major points. "The whole day's going to be like this, isn't it?"

He nodded. "Extravagance and pampering until you just can't take another minute of it. I wouldn't blame you at all if you broke down in tears while having to choose between the lobster and the filet mignon."

"I'll be too busy watching the game. You remember. Dodgers? Baseball?"

"Excuse me, who won the trivia contest?"

"By one point."

"One point was all that was needed."

She had to give it up and smile. "Conceited much?"

Paul turned more toward her. He was in his version of casual—jeans that fit him to perfection, a T-shirt that had to be a size smaller than was wise—the better to show off his shoulders and impeccable abs. He had a baseball cap on the seat across from them and she wondered if he'd risk ruining that scruffy, terribly chic do by putting it on. He was a living, breathing Abercrombie & Fitch ad.

"Somehow," he said, "I doubt you'd have been the model of humility if you'd won."

"I would have been so gracious you'd have choked on it."

He folded his arms across his chest. "I rest my case."

Gwen shook her head, thinking he was right. It wasn't all that bad. If she let herself, she might have a very fine time today. She'd always wanted to watch the game from the suites, and here was her chance. She didn't want to waste it worrying about Paul's motives. If he was being a louse, she'd find out soon enough. The opposite might take longer, but eventually his true colors would be visible. For now, all she had to do was relax. Enjoy the swag. Why not?

"You gave in pretty quickly. I'm worried."

"Don't be. I decided you were right. I've never gone to a game in a limo. It smells very good."

He laughed, and oh, shit, she'd coached herself over and over in preparation, but it was all for naught. He melted something inside her, something she wanted excised, please, as quickly as possible.

How mortifying after being *her,* for God's sake, to be taken in by beauty.

Not only was it wrong, it wasn't fair.

"For someone who's decided to have fun, that's quite a scowl."

She smiled, trying to mean it. "How come you know so much about baseball?"

He seemed as surprised at the question as she was for asking it. "Loved the game since I was a kid. I played all through school. At one point, I hoped to go all the way, but wasn't good enough."

"I'm surprised. I figured you were fabulous at everything."

"That's what my parents counted on, but it's not true. I've always been into sports, though. Basketball, rowing, football, for a while at least."

"Do you still play?"

"Pickup games at the gym, golf, tennis."

"You should have clicked more with my brothers."

"I was preoccupied." He reached into the conveniently placed ice bucket and pulled out a bottle of Heineken. "Beer?"

"I need to pace myself. I have to have a couple of brews watching the game or my boys don't stand a chance."

He nodded. "Then by all means. I have some water in here, I think."

"That's okay. I'm good."

"Do you play? Sports, I mean?"

"We have a company softball league. We also play touch football, and we bowl, depending on the season."

"Sounds as if you do a lot with your coworkers. Anything outside the fold?"

"Not much. The job takes up so much time. It's a very competitive field."

He popped the top on his beer and settled back, one

leg crooked and on the seat. "Is it all science geeks or do you headhunt for other talent?"

"We have different divisions. We're one of the top firms in the world, actually. Offices all over the place. Mostly finance, the sciences and high tech."

"How did you end up there?"

"I majored in chemistry and business. I'm not terribly thrilled with research, so this seemed right."

"Chemistry, huh?"

She nodded. "I like knowing how to blow things up."

Paul laughed. "And how often do you put that knowledge into practice?"

"Not as often as I'd like. It's comforting, however, to know I could if I wanted to."

He held up his beer. "Hear, hear. I can think of several things I'd like to blow to smithereens."

She relaxed a bit more, sinking into the soft leather and the smooth ride. If she could just stop thinking about how damn pretty he was, she felt sure she could have herself a banner day.

PAUL OFFERED Gwen the best seat of the bunch. Not that they weren't all great, but this one, it was primo. He never gave that seat to the women who came with him, knowing they wouldn't appreciate it, but Gwen? Oh, yeah. She got it.

If only he could stop wishing she was as pretty as her sister.

It shouldn't matter. Not for a friend. Hell, he shouldn't be thinking about it at all. He liked her. He did. Still, the wish kept popping up.

And that damn wish kept reminding him about Friday night with Autumn. They'd gone to the party, and she'd been right. It had been a hell of a gathering, as A-list as they come. She'd been flirtatious all night. Unfortunately, she'd shared the wealth with all the men in the room. Normally, that didn't bother him. Most of his dates understood their power and used it indiscriminately, especially around celebrities. He usually felt an odd pride about that.

Not this time.

He'd been irritated at her blatant sexuality, at her obviousness. When she'd been ready for the final tease with him, he'd been so tired and put off he'd barely tried to get her into bed.

"This is the most amazing place I've ever been," Gwen said, staring down at first base. "And I've been to the Parthenon."

Yep. She totally got it. "You're right. Wait till the game starts. You'll never want it to end."

She tore her gaze from the field to look around. Even though it was one of the smaller suites it could still hold up to twenty guests. Occasionally, he brought that many. Clients and contacts, sometimes his poker buddies. Only once had it been him and a woman, but that had been too distracting. When he came here, he wanted baseball. Pure, simple, as it was meant to be played.

He watched her face as she noticed the screens, with a view from every angle. There was the wet bar and fridge, the hot food station, the round tables behind the front row, each with bowls of peanuts and popcorn and even M&M's. She ran her hands over the arms of the Aeron chair, and he watched her test the lumbar feature, knowing there wasn't a more comfortable seat in the whole damn place.

What he also knew was that the thrills were only beginning. The waiters would come in with all manner of delicious food. Dodger Dogs, naturally, but so much more. The beer was ice-cold on tap, the sound from the announcers piped directly in, the action on the field second only to being on the bench.

When she finally looked at him, her smile changed her face. He'd never seen her look like that before, even when they'd danced.

"Thank you. It's heaven."

"I knew you'd like it."

"I do. I just can't believe all this is just for us."

He shrugged. "I have to do business here on a regular basis during the season. For once, I didn't want to think about anything but the game."

"I don't think I could do business. It would be like working in church."

"Exactly. You ready for your beer, or you want to wait for the first pitch?"

She bit her lower lip and for a moment he saw a family resemblance. Not that he could have said exactly what, but it was there. "I'll wait," she said.

"Whatever you want." He sat back and looked past the park to Elysian Field. Even with the smog, it was a great sight. Man, he loved this place.

Gwen got up, and as she passed him, she put her hand on his shoulder. He looked at her, at her happiness, and he felt as if he'd passed a test. It wasn't the whole match, but it was a start.

Now if he could just figure out why he wanted to win at all.

GWEN LOOKED AT HERSELF in the private bathroom mirror and she had to wonder whose life she was living. It wasn't hers, that's for sure.

The game had ended not ten minutes ago—a four-two victory for her boys. She'd eaten unbelievably fine food, shouted until she'd worried about losing her voice, had laughed far more than seemed plausible. In short, she'd had a great time.

With Paul Bennet.

There were still so many questions that she should be asking, but the truth was, she didn't want to. It was one day. One game. She'd had a blast, and not just because of the game.

She'd underestimated Paul in the brains department. Yes, he still had the whole shallow thing going on, and please, she had to deal with enough of that with her family, but he'd said things this afternoon that made her believe there might be some thinking going on underneath that pretty-suit.

Not that she expected him to win the Nobel or anything, but it was heartening. Mostly because she didn't have to feel quite so guilty about getting all twittery when he looked at her for longer than two seconds.

Her chin dropped to her chest. It was no good. He could have said the most brilliant thing she'd ever heard, and she'd still feel creepy. She was the most hypocritical person on earth, and she didn't deserve to have had this day.

The lyrics from *West Side Story* started spinning in her head. Stick to her own kind was exactly what she needed to do. Which should be easy because this was it. She'd made up for being a bitch at Bats and Balls. He'd done his anthropology assignment, or whatever the hell he was trying to accomplish. Done. The end.

She put on some lip gloss, fluffed her hair to no avail, and returned to the suite.

He stood next to the wet bar, leaning against the fridge, his grin showing off the dimples that were simply overkill of cuteness. "I have one more surprise."

"No. No way. I don't think my heart can take it."

"If you want, we can go down and meet a few of the guys."

She knew exactly what "guys" he was talking about. She'd met two in her life. Derek Lowe and Jeff Kent. She'd stuttered like a fool both times. And neither player had paid so much as a second of attention to her.

But they would pay attention to Paul because he was the kind of man people noticed. The kind of man other men wanted to impress.

The question then became, did she want to subject herself to being the question no one asked, but everyone thought? Did her desire to meet ballplayers outweigh her ability to withstand total disinterest and not a small dose of humiliation?

Screw it. She'd been humiliated before. There were very few opportunities to meet her Dodgers. "Let's go."

He pushed off the fridge and gave her a wink. "This is gonna be great."

Yes, it was. She wasn't going to let any of the small stuff get to her. This was her idea of nirvana, something she'd remember forever.

She followed him down the concourse until they got to a smallish elevator. They rode down alone, stopping only when they reached the clubhouse level. That's when a whole new set of jitters hit her.

"Tell me the truth." She hurried to keep in step with Paul so she could whisper. "Will I look like a total dork if I ask them to sign my program?"

"Hell, no. They live for that stuff. They'd be crushed if you didn't."

"Wow, you are so good at your job."

He laughed as he slowed down a bit. They were reaching the gateway to the clubhouse. Two very large men stood guard.

Paul stopped in front of large man number one. "Paul Bennet."

The guard spoke quietly into his Bluetooth. Then he nodded at Paul as he stepped slightly to the right.

With her heart hammering, Gwen took her first step inside the hallowed space. How many times had she longed to get inside? To hear the pros do their own post-game analysis? She admired so many of them, making sure to focus her insatiable thirst for knowledge on their athleticism, not their personal lives. She might be a groupie at heart, but it was for baseball, not ballplayers.

"Watch your step," Paul said. "There are lots of cables all over the floor. And if you see someone talking near a camera, lie low. No one wants to ruin a take."

She nodded even though she knew pretty much all of what he'd said. She was a native Californian, after all. She'd grown up watching movies and TV shows being filmed. Often on her own street.

They got to the press area and the first person she saw was Takashi Saito, the relief pitcher. Then Nomar Garciaparra, and there was the catcher and her favorite first baseman, and holy crap, this was truly the mother lode. She got her program from her purse along with a pen, pissed she hadn't thought of bringing a black marker.

Paul grabbed her hand as he slipped between a newscaster and her boom man. Even though she expected the cables, she almost tripped twice as they maneuvered through the tightly packed space.

He stopped right next to Dylan Hernandez, one of her favorite sportswriters, and waited while he interviewed Joe Torre.

Gwen tried to see everything at once. There were simply too many choices. Too many things she wanted to say to each of the players. Too big of a lump in her throat to even say boo.

The interview ended and Paul stepped right up to the Dodgers manager. "Joe, great game."

Torre shook his hand. "How you doing, Paul."

Gwen could hardly believe he was on a first name basis with the freakin' manager.

"There's someone I'd like you to meet. I know it doesn't sound possible, but she's a bigger fan than I am."

Paul stepped to her side, put his hand on the small of her back to gently urge her forward. "This is Gwen Christopher. You have any questions about your team, I'll bet the farm she knows the answer."

She stuck out her hand and she supposed it was shaken, but she was too busy trying not to act like a doofus. "It's a great pleasure to meet you, sir."

"Sir? You call me Joe."

They said some things, things she knew she would want to remember, but nothing was getting through. It was Paul who had Joe sign her program. Then it was Paul herding a bunch of players in her direction. Each of them seemed delighted to meet her. Of course, Paul made her sound like the greatest baseball expert in the history of the game, and she was frankly too shell-shocked to correct him.

In the end, she'd met almost the whole lineup; her program was so precious to her she'd save it from a fire before her best friend.

By the time he called for the limo, she felt drained, exhausted and so damn happy she was beside herself. The parking lot was mostly deserted, which made sense as the game had ended two hours ago.

She turned to Paul. "I—"

He nodded. "I know."

"But—"

"I know."

"And you—"

"Seriously. I completely understand."

But he didn't. He couldn't. It was one of the greatest times of her life. It was... It was... She grabbed hold of his head, pulled him down and kissed him as if he was Elvis, George Clooney and Sandy Koufax, all rolled into one.

When she let him go, he seemed a little startled. Maybe more than a little. Which made her feel like an idiot and, dammit, why had she ruined this perfect—

"Well, damn," he said, his sly grin growing. "You're welcome."

8

PAUL GLANCED AT his dashboard clock, then at the traffic he was stuck in, wondering whether he should turn around and go home.

For a Monday, his day had gone well. In fact, it was the antithesis of last week. He'd gotten a prime gig for one of his sports clients, saved the internationally famous ass of one of his celeb clients and he'd had a phone call from his mother in Florida where they were actually pleasant to each other.

After work he'd gone to the gym. As he'd hit the showers he realized he didn't want to go home and he didn't want to go to a club. He wanted to play baseball trivia. With Gwen. If he could win twice…

They'd had a good time yesterday at the ballpark. And her friends hadn't seemed to mind him crashing last week. If he didn't get all high school about it, no one would think a thing. Besides, he had that gift for Gwen's friend.

He moved another foot, then another, and for a few minutes there it looked as if he might make it in time to chat before the trivia began. But it being L.A. and it being a day ending in Y, traffic bogged down yet again.

He put on the radio, to the newest station on his rotation, National Public Radio. It had surprised him, how he'd gotten caught up in so many discussions that had nothing to do with the business. Tonight they were talking about happiness. A professor from Harvard had written a book on the subject. The program turned out to be interesting and if it hadn't been so late when he got to Bats and Balls, he'd have listened to the end.

Instead, after grabbing his baseball cap from the backseat, he headed inside, optimistic that this decision had been a good one.

His gaze went straight to her table. There she was. Gwen hadn't noticed him yet. She was busy talking to Holly. From the excitement on Gwen's face, he was pretty sure she had her copy of Sunday's program laid out on the table. He wondered if she'd laminated every page yet.

Ah. He'd been spotted. Gwen's head moved up, her eyes locked on to his. For a split second, there was hesitation there, an almost wince, then it was gone. Holly waved him on as she scooted over to an empty seat at the table.

"I told her you'd be here. I even got you a machine, see?"

Holly held it up, a symbol of good faith.

"Thank you." He sat down, squeezing between the two women. "I had to see if I could do it again."

"I wouldn't count on it, big guy," Gwen said. "You got lucky last week."

"If I were a gentleman, I'd agree with you. But the hell with that. I trounced your ass."

Gwen's eyes narrowed, but she had trouble maintaining the scowl. "I'll let that go, but only because you introduced me to Saito."

"Phew." He looked around for the waitress, but he'd have to wait.

"God, Paul, Gwen hasn't shut up about yesterday." Holly looked different from last Monday. Ah. Makeup. Mostly around her eyes. And her curly blond hair was pinned up. She must have come right from work. Her blouse and skirt were a bit too dressy for Bats and Balls. "I swear she was stopping complete strangers on the street and telling them how she met her fabulous Dodgers." Holly gave him a very dramatic eye roll. "I mean, really. If it had been Brad Pitt, that would be a whole different story."

"Oh, then you probably don't want this." He put the baseball cap on the table making sure Holly saw Garciaparra's signature.

"Are you kidding me?" She looked from the hat to him, then back to the hat. "This is for me?"

He turned the cap slightly so she could see where it said, "To Holly."

She burst into a ferocious grin, grabbed the hat then leaned over and gave him a big kiss on the cheek.

"You're welcome."

She leaned past him. "Gwen, did you see?"

Paul turned to her. He hoped for…he wasn't sure what, but the look Gwen gave him came damn close. Huh. She must have come right from work, too. She was in pants and blouse, very feminine and nice. Like Holly, she'd done something different with her makeup. Subtle, but well-done. She looked prettier. Had her hair always been that soft blond?

Gwen eyed the baseball cap. "I didn't know you'd gotten that. I, on the other hand, was a complete selfish bitch who thought of no one but myself."

"You weren't supposed to think of anything else. That was my job."

She didn't respond. Simply looked at him for a long while, but he had the feeling there was something important going on inside that brain of hers.

"Anyway," he said when he felt heat creep up his neck. "Where is that waitress? I'm dying for a Heinie."

Gwen laughed out loud. "Knowing this waitress, I'm pretty sure you can get it."

"Heineken. *Heineken*. Jeez, make one little slip of the tongue—"

"I repeat, knowing this waitress…"

Everyone at the table found that one particularly hilarious, which made Paul wonder about this waitress. When he looked back at Gwen, her smile had faded but her interest in him hadn't. It was as if she was seeing him now for the first time. Either that, or he had something weird on his face. "Is everything all right?"

She nodded.

"You keep staring at me."

"Sorry. I keep wondering about you. It's odd to me that you're here."

"I can leave."

"No. I'm glad you're here."

He rolled his eyes a bit. "I'm overwhelmed."

"Stop. I had the best time yesterday. I should have said that first thing. It was a spectacular day."

"It was pretty great. We'll have to do it again, some-time."

She looked down, then past him. Her arm went up to call the infamous waitress, who came over. The woman had enormous breasts. She'd probably tried out for Hooters but the T-shirts wouldn't stretch enough. He'd actually never seen breasts that large in real life.

"Hey, gorgeous," she said, her voice kind of scratchy, as if she'd just come back from her cigarette break. "I sure haven't seen you here before."

Now that he was looking at her face, he saw she was older, maybe early forties. "Heineken for me. And refill the table."

The waitress, Carla according to her name tag, winked at him, leaving a tiny smudge of mascara on her cheek. "A hunk and generous. Ain't that a pisser." She walked off with a sashay that Autumn would have envied.

"Game's gonna start in a few minutes, Newbie," Gwen said. "Better get ready."

"I'm always ready."

Gwen's look told him he'd better watch the clichés. Funny, that line would have garnered a deliciously sa-lacious response from Autumn. Or from most of the women he knew.

This was a different crowd with different sensibili-ties, and he felt like a foreigner learning the language.

It was weird, too, because he'd been in all kinds of social situations. With Yale professors, multimillionaires, CEOs, even minor royalty. Yet none of that experience helped him here.

Maybe it was because they all worked together? No, he'd hardly spoken to any of them, except Gwen and Holly. In fact, Holly didn't make him feel this way.

It was Gwen, then. She made him feel awkward. He never felt awkward. His job, in fact, was to make other people feel awkward. Or comfortable. Or whatever he damn well wanted them to feel. Now that the shoe was on the other foot, he looked at his talent in a new light.

"Hello?"

Paul's gaze snapped up to meet Gwen's. "Sorry, what?"

"Log in if you want to play."

He turned his attention to the machine, and a few moments later, to the game. And his drink. The other people at the table as they thanked him for the round. Anything but Gwen.

HER MOUTH WAS OPEN, but nothing was coming out. Mostly because she couldn't believe what she'd just heard. Holly, the woman previously known as Gwen's best friend, had just told Paul that she couldn't drive Gwen home. Despite the fact that she'd driven them both to work. Despite the fact that they lived in the same apartment complex. The excuse was obviously fake, but did that stop her?

"I'll be happy to take her home," Paul said. "Even though she beat me."

"By two points," Holly said, pushing in her chair and fitting her purse strap on her shoulder, the better to make her escape. "I have to run. Thanks, Paul. See you tomorrow, Gwen. Bye."

So now she was standing next to Paul with nothing but a giant slice of awkward between them.

"It's no big deal. It's not as if you live in Connecticut."

"I don't want to inconvenience you especially since you had no choice."

He pushed his seat in, picked up his machine and Holly's, and they left. "I don't mind."

"Thanks."

As they passed Carla, she gave Paul a lascivious grin. Paul barely noticed.

He made the lights of his Mercedes flash with his remote as they hit the parking lot. It wasn't as warm as it should have been in April.

Paul glanced at her as they circled a behemoth truck. "I've got a jacket in the car."

"Thanks, I'm fine."

They reached his car, and he was very gentlemanly, as always, and yet the touch of his hand on the small of her back made her shiver. It was becoming something of an issue, these butterflies. Whether his hand landed on her arm or her back, it didn't seem to matter. Alarmingly, tonight, in the middle of the game, all it had taken was meeting his gaze. She'd like to blame it on his looks alone, but even she'd stopped believing that. Something was happening here, and she had no idea what to do about it.

Once he was behind the wheel, he started the engine and the heater at the same time. The radio came on, too. She recognized the voice from NPR, but he turned that off before she could identify a topic.

"NPR, huh?"

"Yeah."

"I'm a fan, too."

He got them out of the lot and on the way to her place with a minimum of fuss. She stole glances as he drove, the silence in the car not all that uncomfortable, except for, well… She put her hand on her tummy. It occurred to her that things had changed yesterday. He'd been so thoughtful. Gracious. Downright adorable. Dammit. And then today when he'd given that cap to Holly. She sighed. Baseball had leveled the field. There was a common ground between them and yep, that had taken their relationship into a whole new direction.

So much so, that she hadn't thought about her sister more than a couple of times tonight. The evening had been really fun. Winning had been great, yes, but that wasn't all of it. He'd laughed at Steph's jokes, and Kenny's, too. He'd been made fun of, and he'd accepted the ribbing with humor.

Yet, was he worth knowing? Outside of baseball, was there anything in him that she could admire? Did it matter?

They pulled into her apartment complex just as she decided that it did matter if she were to become friends with him. She didn't take friendship lightly.

He found a parking spot pretty close to her apartment. As she grabbed the door handle, he turned to her. "Are you happy?"

She stopped. Debated laughing off the question, but didn't. "Yeah. For the most part, I am. Why?"

Paul turned off the engine. "Do you think it's because you're close to your colleagues?"

She exhaled, curious. "That's part of it, I guess."

"What else?"

"I haven't thought about it all that much. I like my work, but it's not my whole universe. I'm usually busy. I play trivia, I go to old horror flicks, my book club once a month. I watch way too many games, but I guess it doesn't matter because who cares? I don't spend a lot of time dwelling."

"Huh," he replied, as if she'd said something he hadn't expected.

"Why?"

He leaned back a little, staring at her in the semidark. "I'm damn busy, too. I love my work. I have most everything I could want. The car, the house, the women, the toys. But I don't think I'm very happy."

"You don't *think* you are?"

"Okay. Gun to my head? No. Don't ask me why, but that's a very difficult thing to admit. I should be happy. I've got it made."

"Have you felt this way for a long time?"

"Nope. I used to love every second of my life. I'm not even sure when it started to lose its shine. But the parties aren't quite so fabulous, the wins don't give me that jolt as often."

She could tell it was true. Now that she could really see past the handsomeness, there was a sadness in his eyes. There was a decision to be made here. One that led them right off that predictable baseball-loving path. Did she want that? It seemed she did. "Come in. I'll make us coffee."

He smiled. "I'd like that."

IT TOOK A BIT OF TIME to make the coffee and get settled on the couch. He sat at one end, she at the other, but since the couch was curved it made for easy conversations. She'd only put on the mood lighting and as she sat back against her pillows Gwen felt better about her decision to ask him inside.

Yesterday in the clubhouse and tonight at the bar had helped her to see Paul as a person. She'd been so ready to dismiss him as someone empty, someone like Autumn. It hadn't been easy to admit that she had the same kind of prejudice as the people she disliked the most, but there it was.

Without knowing a lot more about him, she couldn't say if the two of them could be friends, yet she was a lot more willing to find out. For him to admit his dissatisfaction with his life was a big deal. It made her like him more than their trip to the ball game.

"This is great," he said, holding up his coffee mug. "Thanks."

"No problem. Tell me something. Was there an event that got you thinking about all this?"

He didn't seem to mind that she'd brought them round to their earlier conversation. "Nothing that stands out. Although I was listening to this guy who wrote a book about happiness."

"Dan something?"

"Yeah. Dan Gilbert. Harvard guy, but I won't hold that against him. He said that the things we think are going to make us happy usually don't. Not for the long run."

"Right, right. That we tend to use our imaginations to predict the things that will make us happy, when we'd be better off using outside resources. Other people who've gone through the experience."

"That's it," he said. "The part that got me was how he talked about how our world is built on the supposition that more material goods equals more happiness. Not that I hadn't heard that before, but it's a damn hard concept to dismiss. Anyway, he also said that the happiest people were those with strong social connections. Family and friends. Like you have."

"I'm not close to my family at all."

"No, but you've created an alternative in your co-workers. I see how you all interact. It's not like that for me."

"Because you're the boss?"

"That's some of it, but not all. I suppose I could have made an effort to make friends with other CEOs."

"But?"

He put down his cup. "Let me tell you about my poker night. I go once every month or so, if I can. Nothing too formal because we're all busy, successful guys. We've known each other for years. And every single time I'm there, it ends up being a pissing contest."

"Kind of like playing baseball trivia?"

He sighed. Picked his mug up. "Yeah. Kind of like that."

"What would you want it to be?"

He took a sip first, then said, "I watched Holly play tonight. Half the time, she didn't even bother to select an answer, even though she had a one-in-five chance of being right. She got too involved in talking, or laughing, or just watching. And I don't think it's just because she

didn't have a chance at winning. She was there to so-
cialize. She won because she was there."

"I don't see that as a solution for you. There's no way
you could go to that bar on Monday night and ignore
the play. You're too competitive."

"Maybe I don't want to be. Not all the time, anyhow. Maybe I'd like to go to a party and not see how
many new contacts I can score. I enjoyed yesterday so
much, I didn't care who won. Well, not much. I wanted
you to have a great day. That was it. The whole goal."

She felt something inside, another shift she hadn't
expected. She mattered to him. Everything he'd done
since the party had shown her that, and yet she still found
it unbelievable. "You did an extraordinarily good job."

"I wasn't… Thanks. The point is, I couldn't tell you
the last time my agenda wasn't about winning. And I
suppose I did win, but it was different. I felt fantastic
last night. After I dropped you off, I went home. I read,
watched a little TV, went to bed. I haven't felt as good
or slept as well in ages."

"Wow. Maybe you should keep doing that."

His grin was teasing and warm. "Taking you to
Dodger games?"

She smiled back. "Stepping outside your comfort
zone. Building a new social network."

"I don't know. It's not easy."

"I have to give it to you. You're sure trying."

"I am. It's so unlike me. This isn't the kind of thing
I do. I've never had to. I was always part of whatever
social group I wanted. All through school I had the right

friends, I was in the right sports, the top fraternity. This is outside of my experience."

"That's what I don't get. Why now?"

He shook his head, then his gaze caught hers. He stared at her for a long time, the expression on his face changing from confusion to something more intense and unsettling.

"What?" She broke the connection, suddenly uncomfortable with how he was making her feel.

"I think about you a lot."

She had to put her mug down before it slipped from her fingers. "Me?"

"Yes, you. It would be a lot smoother of me to make something up, but I don't want to do that. I'm not on sure ground here, so forgive me. I don't think I've known anyone like you."

"I'm not that unique."

"I doubt it. Maybe the world is filled with people who are pragmatic and sensible and sure of themselves without having to win all the time. You love sports, but you don't play games."

Paul stood up and she could see the tension in his body. His shoulders were tight; he rubbed his hands together as he paced on her pale Berber carpet.

She felt badly for him. This had to be difficult, questioning the dream life he'd built for himself. "Do something, then. Who was it that said if you always do what you always did, you'll always get what you always got?"

He stopped, came back to the couch, only this time he sat right next to her. His expression was expectant and the scent of him faint but familiar, reminding her of the night they'd slept together. "I am doing something. I'm here. I keep coming back to you. But I know you don't want me."

She looked at her hands. "I wouldn't go that far."

"Not that you said it out loud, but I know you don't believe I'm someone worth knowing."

"I…" That was exactly what she'd thought, but if she could do it again, she'd have responded differently.

He touched her, his hand warm on hers. It made her look at him again, to see the sincerity in his gaze. "Give me a chance."

She had to swallow the lump in her throat. The unsteady beat of her heart. "I don't know what that means."

He leaned toward her, close enough for her to feel the warmth of his breath. For a second, she thought he was going to kiss her. Instead, his words were quiet, humble. "I love horror movies. And playing softball. I've never been in a book club, but I'd give it a try. I want to be in your life. It's crazy. I don't get why. But you're the key."

9

PAUL COULD TELL he'd made her uncomfortable. He felt like a fool for talking like this, to a woman he hardly knew, but he was also sure that if he didn't say it tonight, he'd convince himself that he was nuts. That all he needed was to get laid a whole lot more and think a whole lot less. He knew that, and something told him if he didn't act, if he didn't put himself on the line right now, he would be sorry. The type of sorry that doesn't ease up with a drink or two.

It was one of the scariest things he'd ever done. Embarrassing as hell. There was nothing concrete he could point to as the cause or the reason. But it felt as real as it gets.

"I don't know what to say." Her gaze met his. "What I do know is that we're from very different worlds. I don't understand a lot about who you are. I admit it. I've probably assumed too much about you, and that's not fair."

"For instance?"

She shook her head.

"I can take it."

After a moment when he thought she might tell him

to forget it, she nodded once. "In my experience, people who are very attractive seem to live on a different planet. It's earth, but it's rarefied. I understand it, honestly."

"Rarefied?"

She nodded, knowing she needed to find the right words. "We're wired to admire beauty. It all goes back to the survival instinct and procreation, but that's not the world I live in, either. I come from a family of exceptionally good-looking people and I've seen how things are easier for them. They got away with amazing things. Their choices were vast. And it gave them all an attitude of entitlement. Scratch the surface of any one of my darling brothers and sisters and you've pretty much reached the other side. There's no *there* there."

"Wow." He exhaled heavily. "Okay," he said. His gaze hadn't wavered from her. "That's not all, is it? There's something that you don't particularly want to say."

He was right. Her theories were her own, but they'd been with her a long time, and dammit, he'd asked. "Mostly, I think what's lacking is compassion. It's not their fault. Compassion comes from pain. And while they've all had their ups and downs, not one of them has ever gone through hell and come out the other side, stronger for the experience."

He wanted to tell her he'd been through hell plenty of times, but he hadn't. She was right about having it easy. People had always seemed to want him to succeed. And for most of his life, that had been enough. More than enough. "I'm guilty of everything you said. I can see how you'd assume I wouldn't be enough for you."

She blinked at him and he was beginning to know

that look. She was thinking about what he'd said, thinking deeply. "I'm not foolish enough to pretend that the lens I've looked through isn't muddy. I'm no paragon, myself. I spent years and years living with jealousy and bitterness. It was hard being the ugly one."

"You're not—"

She stopped him. "We're being honest here, remember?"

"Okay. I swear. I'm being honest. You don't look like the rest of your family. But you're not ugly."

"Paul."

"Hey. I don't want to get sidetracked here, but dammit, I'm not lying to you. I'm the first to admit I'm shallow as hell, but even I can see how lovely your eyes are. How when you smile, your whole face lights up. I find you...arresting. But let's get back to me while I'm still brave enough to ask. Do you believe I'm destined to be this shallow forever? Can you even consider that there might be more to me than you think there is?"

She didn't answer, only this time, he didn't see her telltale blinks. He felt a hopelessness that filled him with dread. This was ridiculous. He tried to get up, but her hand caught his and she held him steady.

"I think you can be anything you set your mind to."

He looked at her again, trying to see beyond the words. Her eyes glistened, and her mouth quivered just a bit. This was new. Gwen wasn't sentimental and she wasn't shy about telling it like it was, which left him...

Confused.

"You're not shallow," she said. "I'm the one who misjudged. I never expected—"

He shook his head. "You think *you're* surprised."

He got a smile for that.

"So you think there's a chance. That we could be friends, I mean."

"There's a chance."

He sat back on the couch, slouching awkwardly but not wanting to move away from her. "I don't have an act two, you know. No clue what to do next."

"Have you considered writing about it?"

"Me? God no."

Her laughter changed the air. "No writing, then. How about just doing what you're doing?"

"And what would that be, exactly?"

"Reading articles that have no opinion on Britney Spears. Coming to trivia night. I do believe there might be a space for you on our softball team, if you can find the time."

He squeezed her hand. "So that's a no about the book club, right?"

"Tell you what. I'll get you a copy of the book we're reading this month. After you've finished it, you let me know if you're interested in joining us."

"Is it about Britney Spears?" he asked.

"Amusing," she said archly. "Seriously. That was amusing."

"Yeah, yeah. But really. Is it fiction?"

"It is," she said.

"Is it thick?"

"Very."

He sighed. "Bring it on. I can't promise anything, but what the hell."

"No expectations. Some of my closest friends don't share my taste in books."

He narrowed his eyes, letting her know this was important. "Are you into Japanese horror?"

"God, yes. I loved *Ju-on*. Hated the American version."

That made him sit up straight. "Yes. American directors don't know what the hell they're doing when it comes to that moody stuff. And I don't consider torture porn to be horror."

She lifted her hand for a high five, which he obliged, but it made him laugh.

"What?"

"Nothing. You just keep on surprising me is all."

"Sweetie, I don't hold a candle to you in the surprise department. You pretty much took my breath away tonight."

"Yeah?"

She nodded as she stood, pulling him up with her. "Yes. It's late. And I have to be bright and perky tomorrow morning."

"Interviewing some new hot scientist?"

"Yup." She led him to the front door. "He's got mad physics skills."

"But can he kick your ass at baseball trivia?"

"That's the first question of the interview."

He laughed.

"Thank you," she said.

"For what?"

"Doesn't matter. Just…" She stepped up to him to kiss his cheek.

He took hold of her shoulders and turned. Her lips

met his. Just like back in that hotel. Only, he wasn't drunk or hungover.

She pulled away, but only for a second. When she kissed him back, it was the real deal, even if he didn't understand why.

Pushing aside all the questions and doubts, he decided to enjoy the moment. The softness of her lips. The way she gasped when he tasted her tongue.

The night had been filled with wonders, but this one topped them all.

He wanted Gwen. Not just to be his friend, but to…

Oh, shit.

IN A DAZE Gwen wandered through the living room, picking up the mugs on the coffee table. Tonight had shocked her in so many ways, it was hard to know where to begin. No, that was a lie. The kiss had taken over her brain. The kiss had evidently startled him as much as it had her. When she'd pulled back, his eyes had been wide-open, staring at her.

For God's sake, she'd kissed him back. With enthusiasm. It had felt amazing and sexy and his hands on her shoulders had made her shiver right to her toes. In fact, she wouldn't have objected if the kiss had gone on a lot longer.

She found herself in the kitchen, several feet away from the sink. She didn't remember walking in there. Setting her mind to it, she put the mugs in the dishwasher, turned off the lights and headed for her bedroom.

Still in something of a trance, she got ready for bed, rehashing things he'd said to her tonight. His determination to be in her life was as troubling as it was flattering. It had all been much simpler when he'd been handsome but dumb.

There were a number of things that attracted her to a man, and one main ingredient was depth. She'd had enough of shallow in her early years. Now she looked for kindness, intelligence, humor and compassion. She'd noticed Paul's kindness at the dance, and even his humor, but she'd written him off on the other must-haves. It had never occurred to her that he could be intelligent, despite his degree and his business acumen. Perhaps if he hadn't been seeing Autumn—

Autumn. Did she know what Paul was up to? That didn't seem likely. Autumn would find this whole business unbelievable and distasteful. Not that Gwen gave a particular damn, but it just brought home the utter weirdness of the situation. Paul Bennet wanted to be in her book club? If that wasn't some cosmic joke…

Paul Bennet had kissed her. On purpose. Her. And she'd kissed him back.

She concentrated on changing into her sleep shirt, then managed to wash her face without zoning out. However, the minute she slipped between the sheets, it was all Paul.

Ridiculously, there was the tiniest temptation to let her thoughts wander to the unlikeliest road she could imagine. That of Paul and her as a couple.

It made her laugh, it was so silly, but she was alone and it was dark, and would she consider being his partner? Sharing her life with him?

No. It couldn't happen. Sure, he could come to trivia and softball games, and even in bizarro world, her book club. She could see all of that. What she couldn't see was her in his universe. Where it was all Autumns and they were all shallow and there were cocktail parties where people talked about movie stars as if they were somehow meaningful. Where beauty was the main commodity, the strange quirk of genetics and makeup that worked magic on a camera.

There was nothing about Paul's world that held any interest for her. Paul might be trying to expand his horizons, but she knew he was the exception. Which made his quest all the more strange.

He would get no points for this trip outside the fold. No one would admire him for wanting more. To that crowd, the only more that mattered was monetary. Bigger cars, flashier clothes. Excess made art form.

While she would admit that she was attracted, okay, strongly attracted, to Paul, it was a limited attraction. Not her idea of a life partner. In fact, she'd been narrowing that ideal for a long time. One critical issue was that she and her unknown perfect mate would have common values. She wasn't all that particular about religion or political affiliation per se, yet it mattered a lot that her eventual guy saw the world through a familiar lens. In all the successful relationships she'd been privy to, the couples had been more alike than opposites.

She couldn't imagine Paul and her finding that. She supposed some people might base an entire relationship on the love of sports, but that wasn't enough for her. And it wouldn't be enough for him.

Ah, who cared. Not a chance either of them wanted

to be together like that. And only a tiny chance that they both wanted to pursue a more sexual relationship.

The mere thought of it made her blush. But after that kiss, she couldn't discard the whole notion, could she?

Would it be so horrible to make love to Paul?

She turned over, sticking her left hand under her pillow, knowing she hadn't asked the right question. The one that really mattered.

Would she be too self-conscious to make love to Paul?

God, she wanted it not to matter. She hated shallowness so much, and yet she couldn't deny that him being so much better-looking had an impact.

All these years, when she'd said looks didn't matter, had she been telling the truth?

She sighed, wishing none of this had happened. Wishing Autumn had never sent him to take her to the party. Wishing…

Wishing she could stop thinking, and just kiss him one more time.

GWEN WAITED outside the little theater, her hands in her sweater pockets, wondering if this evening was a good idea. Paul would be there any minute, and she would prefer to have her game face on by then. If she could decide what her game was.

The Rialto was playing a double bill of Japanese horror. *Ju-on* and *Ringu*. The perfect safe meeting space for two potential friends.

Only, there was the whole after to deal with. It was always better if there were beverages and discussions following favorite films. That seemed safe, but Gwen knew that once the conversation wound down, Paul would walk her to her car. He just would. And that was the moment she was so troubled about.

In the three days since he'd been to her house, they'd spoken on the phone five times. The first, he'd asked her for the name and author of another book she'd mentioned. The second, he'd called about the softball team, and found out that he couldn't play until next Wednesday. The third, he'd started with a question about the book, then admitted he just wanted to talk. That call had lasted one hour and twenty-two minutes.

Today he'd called twice. Once to ask her if she'd like to see the movies, and again to ask her if he should pick her up. She'd had that answer on the ready.

She enjoyed him on the phone. Startling, because she really wasn't much of a phone person. Holly knew that. Their calls were brief and to the point. If either of them needed to really talk, they got together. It was great.

In fact, all of her friends knew about her phone habits. Only, Paul had made her change the rules. Being on the phone with him was easy. Not in the least simple, but easy.

Every time her phone rang, even at work, her heart sped. Whatever thoughts she'd had vanished and it was all she could do not to leap to answer the damn thing. The thing was, she wasn't like this. Never had been. Even in the worst of her teen angst, she hadn't been like the other girls who couldn't seem to manage a single thought outside of their past, present or future boyfriends. Gwen hadn't understood it then, and she sure as hell didn't understand it now. It was weird. A little bit wonderful. But troubling, too.

"Hey, you look worried. Did you think I'd be late?"

She turned to look up at Paul and her smile came without a thought. So did the flutters plaguing her so often these days. "No, I was just thinking about stuff."

"Dangerous occupation. It always gets me into trouble."

"We've got just enough time to get popcorn and good seats."

He glanced at his watch, some terribly expensive army-looking thing. "Half an hour."

"I said *good* seats." She took out two tickets from her pocket. "See? I knew you'd be here on time."

"I was going to get those."

"You may buy the popcorn, which I assure you will be more expensive. I love my popcorn."

"A giant tub?"

"For me, yes. You may get what you like."

He laughed. "A giant soda to go along?"

She handed the tickets over to the nice man at the door. "Nope. Medium, diet. With the popcorn, make sure they put the butter on halfway through, then again at the end. No skimping."

He touched her back as he escorted her to the candy counter. Just a touch, something one friend would do with another friend, no biggie, and yet it was a biggie, it was giant because she reacted like… She reacted foolishly.

The popcorn saved her. Paul ordered, not even blinking at her request for diet soda. He got himself a large popcorn, no butter. Fool. He clearly didn't understand movies the way she did.

Inside, the theater was already a quarter full, mostly with teenagers. A few older folks sat in the far corners, but she wanted dead center. So did everyone else, but they ended up with decent enough seats.

Once settled, purse and sweater were put aside, popcorn and napkins on her lap, cup in the holder. It was perfect and she sighed contentedly.

"Yeah," he said, his voice showing much pleasure. "How many times have you seen these two?"

"Three and two, respectively. I only hope that the film stock is decent. This theater can be hit-and-miss."

"I got them both on DVD, but I prefer seeing them here. They're scarier."

She nodded as she dug into the great bucket of buttery goodness. "I also love the coming attractions. It's all good."

"So is the book you gave me."

"You still like it?"

"No. I like it more. It kept me up too late last night. And tomorrow, I've got a showing to go to, and I'm resenting it. I almost called to cancel, but it's my company, my party. So the book will have to wait."

"I understand. You should get an audiobook next time. Listen to it in traffic. You'll get through it faster."

"Good—" He stopped, when the lights dimmed. "Good," he said again, but it was an entirely different sentence.

Gwen was terribly aware of him until fifteen minutes into *Ju-on*. By then, she was wrapped up in the story, anticipating the scary bits. She kept eating her popcorn, pausing just before something bad happened. That was the fun of multiple viewings—no danger of choking.

Then, about ten minutes later, Paul touched her hand. The underside. After a moment's hesitation, he slipped his fingers between hers.

She hadn't had anyone hold her hand in a movie in years. If anything, dates had put their arm around her to snuggle. This was infinitely sweeter. She felt like a teenager again—no, younger than that. There was an innocence to his move, a tiny step where nothing else would have worked.

Despite the gasps of fear that filled the theater, the ominous music, she looked at Paul to find him looking at her.

He smiled. Tossed some popcorn in his mouth, then turned back to the screen.

She wasn't worried about the ending anymore. Not of the movie or of the night. He'd just told her she was safe.

And then with a jolt she realized that wasn't true at all.

10

GWEN CLOSED HER FRONT DOOR, dropped her purse and sweater on the table, then flopped onto her couch with a satisfied sigh. She couldn't have asked for a better night.

They'd held hands for the rest of the movie and for all of the second. Her fingers had been squeezed during the scariest bits and her palm tickled once for no reason at all. They'd gone to a nearby coffee shop after, where he'd had a piece of chocolate cake, which, she pointed out, negated his low-cal popcorn. He'd been unimpressed with her logic as he'd devoured every bite.

If she hadn't known better, she would have called it a date. But it wasn't. For heaven's sake, they were just beginning their friendship and neither had spoken of anything more. Friendships were good. Lovely. And the hand-holding was nothing more than…what? Maybe her definition of friendship might need some refinement.

But it was late and she was foolish. Time to get ready for bed. She didn't hurry, though. She went into the kitchen to put her breakfast dishes into the dishwasher, her thoughts turning to the end of their night.

As she'd predicted, he'd walked her to her car, but just as she'd unlocked her door, he'd gotten a phone call from a client. Voilà. No kissing awkwardness. A perfect ending all the way around.

She looked at her hand, still marveling that she'd been so giddy over such a simple thing. What was happening to her? Her maturity and good sense were going straight down the tubes, and she didn't mind in the least.

Okay, so maybe it hadn't been the absolute perfect ending to their evening. He could have thrown the phone into the bushes, pulled her into his arms and kissed her desperately, swearing his undying—

Uh, wait. That's not at all what she'd wanted. Dramatic, yes, but it would have freaked her out so badly, she'd have run for the hills.

She didn't want him that way. Not in real life. So she had fantasies. So she wasn't immune to the romantic mythos. Yes, even levelheaded women who knew better could still dream about being in a fairy tale, right? That didn't automatically knock off IQ points. It was just part of her girl DNA.

With that settled, she finished cleaning up the kitchen. It was past her bedtime and she didn't do well on less than seven hours. She wished someone would invent a way to get a washed face and clean teeth without actually having to wash or brush. A knock on the door caught her just before her bedroom.

It was past midnight. Who could be knocking at this hour, unless it was Holly? Gwen ran to the door and opened it.

It wasn't Holly.

"Good, you weren't in bed yet. I've been standing out here for ten minutes worrying I'd wake you."

"Paul."

He gave her a wobbly smile. "Never mind. I'll go."

She grabbed his arm. "No, don't be silly. I was just surprised, that's all. Come on in."

He followed her, stopping in the foyer. "The thing is, I didn't really say good-night."

"It's okay. It was business. Something that clearly had to be taken care of."

"Yeah, it did. But you left so suddenly. I wanted to tell you that I had a really great time."

"Me, too—"

He stepped close, took her arm. "That's not what I wanted to say. I mean, I had a great time, but I came here because I couldn't just let it go."

"Let what go? Did I do something wrong?"

"No. Nothing's wrong except I didn't want you to go. I wanted to kiss you good-night."

Her eyes had locked on to his, mesmerized by the look of hunger there. It was the look she'd imagined in the dark of night, under the covers. Not something she ever expected to actually see. It felt…wrong. Heat filled her cheeks and she broke free from his grasp.

"Oh, shit. I'm sorry. I thought…"

"It's fine. I just wonder if it's such a good idea to, you know—"

"No, no. I get it." Paul took a step back, but he looked hurt. "My mistake."

Insecurities she hadn't felt for years stormed inside her. Could it be possible for them to be lovers? Everything in her experience said no, but just looking at him made her want so badly to be wrong. It didn't happen this way. Beautiful women with unattractive men? A staple of TV sitcoms. Beautiful men with women like her? Not unless the women magically turned to swans. That wasn't going to happen to her. Ever. But, oh, God, the way he looked at her.

He still stood frozen, stealing glances that only made him seem less sure. "What do you want?" he asked softly.

"I don't know."

"That kiss the other night. It didn't feel like you hated it."

She closed her eyes for a moment. "You know I didn't."

"Then what? If you want me to leave, I'm gone." He closed the distance between them, and lifted her face to his. "But if you want me to stay…"

"I don't understand this."

"Don't try," he whispered as he stole her breath with a gentle kiss. Then his hands went to her waist, pulling her tight. The kiss changed, leaving no room for misinterpretation.

Gwen's body reacted as if he'd awakened her from a deep sleep. She felt everything so sharply. His chest pressing her breasts, his stomach and thighs against her and most especially the hardening length of his cock.

What was she doing, kissing him back? Sucking on his thrusting tongue, letting herself moan with awakening pleasure? This was wrong in every way. She was smarter than this. Paul was not hers, not for her, not remotely the kind of man who should make her moan outside of a dream.

She pushed against his chest but it was clear she didn't mean it. His coming here, his wanting her had caught her off guard, that's all. It had been forever since someone had been so eager, so determined.

His mouth widened, his tongue probed then withdrew and it was as if they were dancing again, both knowing the steps as if they'd practiced a hundred times. His low moans matched hers in spirit if not in tone, and she found her hips thrusting in that same swaying rhythm.

He drew back, breaking contact, only to stare at her, his eyes dark in the muted light. He took her hands, put them around his neck, and he kissed her again.

Another shock ran through her as it hit her who she was kissing, but just as quickly, her brain turned off, at least the thinking parts. The feeling parts wanted all the attention. More of his hands rubbing her back, more of the taste of him, peppermint slightly on his tongue. She remembered his scent from the hotel bed and it sent urgent messages that made her nipples harden and her knees grow weak.

There was nothing arm's length about this. This was everything she'd hoped for in her most secret heart. It had no chance of ending well, not in the long run, but for tonight? There was a chance.

"I want to make love to you," he said, his lips so close to her own she could taste his breath. "I'd wanted to before, but nothing like tonight. When I watched you drive away, I couldn't get it out of my head."

"It's crazy."

"So what?"

"I… We… Damn," she said, then she kissed him again, knowing the millisecond had passed when she could have sent him home.

The difficulty was keeping the momentum going. If she stopped for the slightest thing she knew she'd find a hundred reasons why she was out of her mind. Clearly, her only choice was to not stop.

She began by moving them closer to the living room. No bedroom, no bed. The couch was fine. Once there, she slipped her hands between them and began to unbutton her blouse. It wasn't easy, but she managed to keep their lips together as she slipped the blouse off, as her hands went to the clasp of her bra.

To his credit, he seemed to understand the whole momentum thing. His hands got busy divesting himself of his shirt in the quickest way possible, then pants, although for that they had to coordinate and bend down as a team.

Dancing. It was all dancing, and she supplied her own music. A tango, of course. There should have been violins and guitars, but her heartbeat would do, that and the sound of breathing, of too-quick inhalations, long held desperate gasps.

Then it all came to a crashing halt.

"What?" he asked, but it sounded like a curse.

"I don't have a condom."

"I do."

"Where?"

"Pocket."

"Thank God." She found his mouth and they dropped the final garments in their separate heaps. It wasn't the most comfortable thing to wait while he found his pocket and the permission-giving condom, but worth it. He pulled her close again as he rose, laughing in triumph even as they continued to kiss.

"Don't think," he said, running his hand down her back so lightly she shivered. "Just feel."

She let him carry her down to the couch, her thigh brushing against his erection. Of course once she was sitting and he stood right in front of her, she had a whole new perspective on things. First, she completely got it that Paul's enthusiasm wasn't intellectual. His erection was impressive. When she could tear her gaze away and look at his naked chest, shoulders, arms and then that face...all she could do was drop her head in her hands.

There was a thump, then his hands were on her knees. She peeked to find him kneeling. "What's wrong?"

"It's no good. You're just too damn pretty."

"You're thinking again. That's not allowed."

She opened her mouth, but he stole her argument by easing her thighs apart.

"Because you're having a difficult time with this concept, I'm going to help you."

Again she tried, but he stopped her with a look. Normally, glares wouldn't shut her up, but his was accompanied by his hands lifting up her legs and slipping them on his shoulders.

"You're allowed to make all the noise you like." He leaned forward, adjusting her position and his. "But no words. In fact, I'm going to make sure you lose the power of speech altogether. So sit back and relax. Let me make you happy."

Naturally, all she wanted was to argue. Until his fingers brushed up her thighs. When he got to the end of the road, he stroked her pussy gently. She closed her eyes as his breath warmed her delicate skin. Her head went back, her hands clutched the couch cushions. He won. So it wasn't her life. She might as well enjoy herself.

The warm breath on the very edge of her thighs narrowed and then it was lips. The tip of his tongue, licking, nipping.

A fingertip slid slightly inside her, moving slowly, just teasing her with the promise of things to come. He nibbled one thigh, then the other, increasing the pressure against her clit so slowly she had to thrust up against him.

He moaned at the movement, rewarding her by concentrating on the one spot with tiny circles.

The nibbles stopped. He used both thumbs to spread her open. She held her breath as he found her clit with the hardened tip of his tongue.

Gwen gasped and her hands moved to the back of his head, fingers running through his thick, dark hair. It was as silky as she'd imagined, but she couldn't focus on him for long. Not while he was doing such incredible things to her.

It had always amazed her how men loved to do this. At least most of the men in her life. She'd never questioned her luck, just accepted it as a delightful bonus. Paul's low moans, his careful attention, his expertise told her this was a treat for both of them.

She just wished she could touch more of him. That body of his called to her. There was so much to explore, so many perfect parts. God, to cup that ass.

He sucked her clit between his lips. Sucked hard. It was an incredible sensation, one that made her cry out, clutch his hair. Straining now, feeling the magic start deep in her body. There was nothing else now but this, needing to come.

He captured her nub between his teeth and flicked the tip of his tongue right there, fast, like a humming-bird's wings.

She let go of him to steady herself as her orgasm broke inside her, touching every muscle, making her see spots behind her closed lids.

She cried out, riding the wave, clutching his head between her thighs. Seconds went by in absolute bliss, then she shifted her butt, away from his tongue, her sensitivity off the scale.

When she opened her eyes, he was staring up at her, pleased with himself, with her. As she watched, he wiped his mouth with the back of his hand, then stood.

His cock glistened, his excitement as clear in his eyes as it was in his jutting erection.

"Sit down," she said.

He didn't question her, which was a good thing. It was her turn to stand. The first thing she did was find the condom. It was on the floor next to her foot. She ripped it open, but didn't put it on him, yet.

Still quivering, she settled before him. He looked unbelievable, sitting on her couch, his legs spread arro-gantly wide, his hips thrusting, his chest heaving. But his gaze made her look away.

She brushed her hands up his legs and thighs until she was able to hold him with both hands. One around his shaft, the other cupping his balls. All she wanted now was to learn the feel of him. To stroke him, to lose herself in texture and heat.

His moan made her glance up. His head had gone back, his mouth slightly open. Her body relaxed as she played with him.

Soon, touching him wasn't enough. She took his crown in her mouth, holding him for a long moment. Then she swirled her tongue.

The sound he made accompanied a tremor, a stiffening of his body, and not just the part she had between her lips. He thrust just a little. She could feel his struggle as he held himself in check.

The taste of him was as unique as his scent. His noises just as singular. She closed her eyes as she licked him, long strokes with the flat of her tongue, all the way down, then switching her hands to his cock as she licked his balls which seemed to please him a great deal. His pleasure infused her with a flush of heat. A sense of power.

"Oh, God, Gwen." His voice sounded as tense as his thigh muscles. "Please."

She lifted her lips. "Tell me."

He touched her face. "Nothing. Everything. Just more."

She grinned and took his crown once more, this time she sucked until he groaned, determined to make him beg.

It happened quickly. He wasn't able to stop the small thrusts. She did everything her mouth could do to him, her fingers playing the counterpoint. It was greed that kept her so busy, to make him thrum in her mouth, to force his gasps.

"Stop, Christ, stop."

She pulled away her lips, although she couldn't let go altogether.

He made her when he leaned forward to capture her arms. "Come, now. Where's the goddamn thing."

She grabbed the condom before he could haul her up. Slipping it on his moist erection made him hiss and the second it was in place, he practically lifted her to her feet.

"Here," he said, letting her know he wanted her on top.

She hesitated, but he wasn't having any of it. He had her on the couch a second later, her knees on either side of his thighs.

"God, I need—" He rose up to kiss her, his tongue fierce as it thrust.

It was both of them she tasted. Even as Paul kissed her savagely until she was poised above him. One hand disappeared from her lower back, and then he grunted and thrust up.

A moment of hesitation, making him strain for more, and then she gave in, not a surrender at all because she wanted him inside her. Filling her.

She rode him, controlling the pace, blessing her Pilates for giving her the strength she needed. His kisses urged her to move faster, harder, but she wouldn't give in, not yet.

Her movements were purposely slow, but quick wasn't the goal. Not when she could make him go insane with her squeezes, with the maddening tempo.

His hands were everywhere. Her back, her breasts. A brief grasp of her hair to steady her, then back to her nipples, where he twirled and flicked, ruining her strategic assault.

Hell, it was no use. All her finesse was gone, and it was all about the finish. Cunning man, he reached between them and found her clit. It did the trick. She was riding him now, full out.

With a suddenness that shocked her, he stopped. "Gwen, look at me."

She shook her head as she squeezed him, urged him to get on with it.

"Look at me," he said, and this time he took hold of the back of her hair. "Please."

His face flushed, he stared at her, into her, as he kept her perfectly still while he thrust again and again until she thought her heart would beat out of her chest.

She watched his expression contort into a mask of pure tension, the fight between his cock and his desire to hold back one more second.

As he lost control, he drew her to him, his staccato thrusts rubbing her clit into an explosion of her own. She held on to him as she trembled, as her body spasmed. He kissed her face, all over, just mad kisses until he found her mouth.

They held each other until their hearts calmed. Until the kisses gentled.

11

PAUL COULDN'T TALK YET, although he was in a lot better shape than five minutes ago. Gwen had settled next to him, dragging a soft throw over their bodies. He had his arm around her and her head was in the hollow where his chest met his shoulder.

"Well, this is a fine how-do-you-do," she said.

He chuckled, never having heard that as an après-sex comment before. "Appropriate, though," he said, feeling that he knew a great deal more about her than before.

"Huh?"

"Nothing," he said, lacking the verbal and mental skills to explain. "Don't expect me to be coherent."

"Fair enough."

"I have to say, for a couch, this wasn't so bad."

"What do you mean?"

He let his hand smooth down her arm. "It didn't scratch up my ass."

He felt her lips curve into a smile.

"First thing I checked out in the department store."

"Dropped trou, did you?"

"It was a major purchase."

His head lifted as he grinned, but he couldn't really

see her face so he let it flop back again. "Popcorn and a treat. Best movies ever."

"It's not what I expected."

"No?"

"We were supposed to be friends."

He lifted his head once more. "Aren't we?"

"We hadn't exactly discussed the benefits package."

He really needed to see her face. He lifted her chin, which upset the balance of things, but had to be done. "Are you sorry?"

The look she gave him was honest, if not quite as satisfying as a whimper and instant denial, but that was Gwen. "I don't know. I don't mean I didn't enjoy it. God, I did. But—" she sat up, tugged the blanket a bit to cover her lap "—I'm not sure where it leaves us."

"Does it have to leave us anywhere in particular?"

Her shrug said as much as her troubled gaze. "I'd like to say no, but that's not how I operate. I'm not a casual sex kind of person."

"Nothing about you is casual."

She poked him lightly with her elbow. "If that was supposed to be a compliment, it sucked."

"It was." He ran a hand over his face, then sat up a bit straighter. "I admire it, though. I like that you have high standards."

"I suppose—no, I don't understand that, either."

"Case in point," he said. "But I'll try to explain. You don't settle, and you expect the best from me. Which makes me want to give you my best. I've never had that with a friend before, benefits notwithstanding. The truth is, somewhere during the past few weeks, I realized I wanted more."

"You didn't say anything."

"I kissed you."

She sighed in the nicest way. "Yes, you did."

"And as I recall, you kissed me back."

This time, he got a nod.

He stroked her face with the back of his fingers. "What do you want?"

She captured his hand and held it there for a moment. "I don't know. I was just getting used to the friendship part."

He thought about that. About what being friends with Gwen had started out as, and how different it was from anything he'd experienced before. It had never occurred to him that he was moving too fast. In his life before Gwen, these things tended to happen quickly, skipping over the friendship altogether. The only exception in recent memory had been Autumn, but she didn't seem to count anymore. It felt as if meeting Gwen had forced a spotlight on Autumn's game-playing, and in that glare, it had lost all its charm.

"Hello?" She looked him in the eyes, waiting.

He wanted the sex. It balanced things for him, but he skittered away from that thought. No, he'd wanted her. "I should have waited."

"Please don't feel bad. I was right there with you. I could have said no."

"That's fair. Tell you what. Let's play it by ear. I'll try to be more focused on the friend thing."

"I like that. I'm still learning so much about you."

"Huh. That's a pretty shallow pool."

"No, it's not. I thought it would be, but you've turned out to be an interesting guy."

"Don't let that get out. It'll ruin my reputation in this town."

She grinned. "We're in Pasadena. You're still safe in Hollywood."

After looking at a face that had changed so much in such a short time, he pulled her into a kiss. Nothing fancy. Just a hope, perhaps that while the whole nine yards might be off-limits, this might not be. Kissing her was something he didn't want to give up.

Finally, she drew away. Pushed some hair back from his forehead with the tips of her delicate fingers. "It's late."

"One thing, and then I'll go."

"What's that?" she asked.

"Friends with kissing, that could work, right?"

She looked at him with those green eyes of hers. He could practically see the debate inside her head. Finally, she smiled, and he knew her answer.

"Yes. Friends with kissing could work."

"Yippee," he said, mocking his own exuberant reaction so she wouldn't get scared and change her mind. "I'll wash up." He stood, left her the blanket, gathered his pile of clothes and went into the bathroom. As he cleaned up, he tried to remember why he'd considered her so plain. Probably the contrast to Autumn. But now that he knew Gwen so well, the scales had shifted. There was little better than winning a smile from Gwen.

Naturally, when he got to the door he wanted to try

the whole friends with kissing thing. Just to make sure they both understood the concept.

Wrapped in her blanket, he tugged her close and kissed her. Not a peck, either, but a long, hot kiss that made them both moan. When he broke away, it was with real regret, but also hope. Oh, yeah. Friends with kissing was a great start. He just prayed he could stand it while he waited for her to see the wisdom of a comprehensive benefit package.

IT WAS FOUR DAYS until he saw her again. Monday night trivia, and of course, he arrived only minutes before the game. She had saved him a seat, and there was a game player waiting, but what he mostly wanted was a beer.

He sat down, pleased to be in the hubbub and chatter of the now-familiar gang from her work. He knew everyone at the table tonight, which was cool.

First thing, he turned on his machine. Second, he leaned over and kissed Gwen a proper hello, although it wasn't nearly the kiss he could have planted on her. Then he went to type in his nickname. When he looked up, no one at the table was talking. In fact, they were all staring at him. With a thunk, he realized that he'd just done a very stupid thing.

He cleared his throat and looked desperately for a waitress as he cast about for some way to fix this. She worked with these people. She clearly didn't want them to know they were kissing friends, and here he'd been so pleased that he'd shown such restraint.

"It's good to see you, too," Gwen said, her voice pleasant, her glare not so much.

His whole face got hot, but when he dared look at her, there was no real anger in her eyes. Braver, he looked at his tablemates. They were obviously bewildered, but no one shot him furious glares or threw anything at him. The last test would be Holly.

She was all shock, but pissed off, too. Not at him, though. At Gwen. Holly leaned over his back, forcing his head down to the table.

He heard Gwen say, "Ouch," and figured Holly had given her a shot in the arm.

"What was that for?" Gwen said.

Holly grunted, but in a feminine way. "You know perfectly well."

"Okay, okay. I'm sorry. We'll talk later, I promise. But the game's starting now, and I think you're killing Paul."

Holly eased up but gave him a shriveling glare. "Some nerve." She gave him a pop, too, and it hurt quite a bit. "She's my best friend. I should have been in the loop."

"Sorry," he said, wishing the beer would get there, wishing he didn't want to rub his arm like a little girl. Glad it was out in the open, and that he could touch Gwen tonight. He'd missed her, even through a ridiculously busy few days. There'd been no reading, no movies, not even any baseball games. Just work, a phone call here and there and some nice memories to put him to sleep.

After the first question came up on the board, Gwen leaned over so her mouth was close to his ear. "Smoothly done, Casanova."

"I'm sorry," he whispered back. "I didn't think."

"I forgive you."

He turned fully to her, the whisper be damned. "Do you now? How magnanimous."

She nodded, pleased with herself.

He leaned toward her, shifting his glance between her eyes and the big board while he moved his hand to his game machine. He made sure she was looking at him, though, when the next question popped. That's when he kissed her again. A long one. If there'd been any doubts before from any of her coworkers, they were dispelled by the smoldering lip-lock. Of course, he answered the trivia question at the same time, and when the answer period was over, he let her go. He couldn't suppress his grin, knowing he'd won on two counts.

She looked up at the board. Then at him. Then she socked him in the other arm. It hurt a lot worse than Holly's punch.

GWEN KEPT HERSELF as calm as possible as the game continued. It wasn't his fault, that kiss, not really. They hadn't discussed the public face of their relationship. Friendship. Besides, it had been a spontaneous gesture that had been not only sweet but a little breathtaking, so she couldn't be mad at him. She'd learned long ago to defuse tricky situations by acting as if they weren't tricky at all. But now that they were pressing buttons, trying to win, drinking beer, in essence back to normal, the gravity of what he'd done hit her.

These were the people she worked with. To most of them, she was the boss, although in her office there wasn't much of a caste system. There was a great deal of camaraderie, but when things got dicey they all knew her word was final. No one objected and the atmosphere at work was mostly jovial, if task oriented.

She'd only brought one man into the fold at all, and that had been on two occasions. Alex had been nice, but mostly a rebound guy, and their dalliance hadn't lasted long.

Paul, on the other hand, had been allowed in on the basis of being her friend. No hint had been given that there was more. Well, Holly had wanted it to be a love affair, but that was Holly. No wonder she was cranky. Gwen wasn't even sure why she'd kept things so quiet.

Although she hadn't seen Paul since that night on the couch, they'd spoken every day. Poor guy, he'd been slammed with work and clients and entertaining, but he still managed to sneak in his daily call.

While it had been nice to speak to him, she hadn't been prepared for dreaming about him. Not just any dreams, either. Vivid, sexy, naked dreams.

Naturally, she didn't tell him. Not when she was so confused about what this thing was between them. At least she still had a grasp on the fact that sexual attraction was not enough. Although it sure felt as if it would be. No, there were issues to be dealt with. Big ones.

For example, the incongruity of the two of them together. Even now Kenny kept sneaking stares, his expression perplexed, although he tried to hide it. And there was Steph, shaking her head with what looked to be disbelief.

Gwen shifted her attention to the game, her drink, anything rather than see the reactions around her. It wasn't a surprise. Come on. She might have a lot of good qualities, but beauty wasn't one of them. It wasn't something she could hide or disguise. What pissed her off was that it had never been a part of her relationships at work. Never.

She pressed the button on her machine, realizing too late it was the wrong name. She swore, not just at her bad answer, but at her concern over what her friends thought. Ridiculous. She had nothing to apologize for. Nothing to feel weird about.

"What is going on with you?"

She jumped at the sound of his voice, so near to her.

"You're going to win," she whispered. "I hate that."

"Get used to it, darlin'. I rock at this."

She gave him a glare, then said, "Cheater" semidisguised as a cough. "You're going to pay for that."

"Oooh, how?" He looked entirely too excited.

"I don't know yet. It won't be the fun kind of revenge, mark my words."

He laughed, which got everyone looking at them. Gwen kissed him, which he really didn't deserve. But what the hell, right? He made her laugh, and he made her happy. If anyone didn't like it, they could just screw off.

FINALLY, PAUL WAS UP TO BAT for the first time.

Gwen stood in the bleachers right next to Holly. She wanted him to knock it out of the ballpark, but barring that, to not strike out. He'd been touted as a ringer. He certainly looked like one. Terribly buff in his T-shirt and jeans, he even managed to make the batting helmet look sexy.

"Go, Paul!" Holly was shouting so loud Gwen had to cover her ears.

"I don't think they heard you in St. Louis."

"I'm just being an excellent teammate," Holly said. "You should be shouting, too."

"I'm encouraging him in my own way."

Holly bumped her shoulder. "He can't see you crossing your fingers."

The pitcher lobbed the ball and it was a swing and a miss.

"That's okay, Paul." Holly shouted again. "Good eye, good eye."

Gwen saw that while his timing was off by a hair, he had real power. As soon as he did connect, the ball would fly out of the park. She crossed the fingers of her other hand.

Another strike.

The whole team was shouting now, at least those not too busy drinking beer from the conveniently located cooler. They were playing against Harland, Inc., a very reputable agency with very nice people whom her crew liked a great deal off the field. The loser had to spring for beer and pizzas after.

At the third pitch she held her breath. A ball. That was okay, but her heart couldn't take this. She wanted to sit down, shut her eyes until it was over, but couldn't. Another pitch and damn! The crack of the bat filled the air and that ball was so far out of there it almost hit a car across the street. A home run!

Gwen shouted like a lunatic. She was so proud of him, it set off every girl hormone in her body.

Then when he came back to the bleachers, panting after running the bases, and swept her into his arms for a kiss, she positively swooned with such happiness that she had no words. Only feelings. Lots of them.

"WHAT'S THIS?"

Paul's secretary placed the brightly wrapped package on his desk. "It just arrived."

"What is it?"

"I believe you're going to have to open the package to find out." Tina grinned at him, then returned to her office.

He had a million things to do today, but he could take a few minutes to open it, right? He tore into the paper and there was his first hint, a rather big one. The name Christopher on a shipping label on the box. What was Gwen up to?

He wrestled with the tape and finally got the box open to find a very well protected, very small reproduction of Venus de Milo.

He knew instantly that he'd assumed the wrong Christopher yet again.

A card was inside the box.

Sweet, Wonderful Paul,
Here I am in Rome with all its great restaurants and fabulous bars, but all I can think of is you. I hate that you haven't called me. I know I've been out of town, but I'm coming home on Thursday. Please, please let's do something wicked. I won't be able to have a good time until I'm with you. I hope you like the Venus.
Love, Autumn

Damn. He'd been putting it off, but that had to end. He'd make lunch plans with her. That couldn't end up too badly, right? Besides, he didn't think it would break her heart not to have him chasing after her. Her ego, maybe, but nothing more.

He needed to tell her what was going on with him and Gwen. Or maybe he should break it off with her first, then tell her about Gwen another time. Knowing Autumn, that seemed the best route.

He placed the Venus, which didn't match the decor in his office or his house, and was pretty shabby in fact, back into the box. Then he hit Gwen's speed-dial number on his phone.

"Gwen Christopher."

"It's me."

"Hey," she said, and he could hear her smile.

"What are you doing tonight?"

"Book club," she said, her voice low and intimate.

They hadn't done more than kiss since that night. He hadn't pressed, she hadn't brought it up. All the same there was a whole lot of simmering going on. "Tonight?"

"Yes, tonight."

"Oh."

She laughed. "I completely understand why you haven't finished the book. It's okay. You've been incredibly busy."

"Yeah, but—"

"No buts. Besides, I don't think you'd love book club. Especially my book club. We tend to go off on tangents. Long ones. Many involve cooking."

"Cooking?"

"Seriously, Paul. Finish the book if you like, but don't think twice about these little meetings. Use tonight to catch up on some sleep. You need it."

"I know what would make me sleep better."

She snorted. "That's such a lie I can't even stand it. Drink some warm milk. Read. Sleep."

He sighed. "I'll try, but I've been putting off a couple things I need to handle. Save tomorrow night for me. I've got a dinner to go to at The Ivy. No big deal…it would be nicer if you were there."

There was a pause, which he figured was work related. Finally, she came back to him. "I wish I could. I don't think that's gonna work for me, though. Anyway, my three o'clock is here. Talk to you later."

With that, she was gone. What had happened? How had a woman he shouldn't even know become so important to him?

12

CHILI'S WAS BUSY, as usual, and the dinner crowd was noisy, still Gwen and Holly had scored a relatively quiet corner booth. It had been too long since the two of them had spent any quality time together. No games, no movies, no work to discuss. Just Gwen's best friend and some good chow.

"I'm having the ribs." Holly put down her menu and shoved it to the middle of the table. "I shouldn't have ribs, but I am. With fries. And a beer."

"I understand completely." Gwen looked for their waitress, who was nowhere to be seen. "I've had too much popcorn and beer lately. So it's a salad and water for me."

"Well, I don't have a man to get naked for." Holly sighed. "I'd totally have salad if it would mean I could order someone like Paul off the menu."

"I'm not getting naked."

Holly's look of shock was like something from a cartoon. "You're not? What's wrong with you?"

"Nothing's wrong. We're just taking it slowly."

"Excuse me, but you're completely insane. Have you looked at him?"

Gwen nodded, wishing they'd at least gotten their

beverages before this subject had come up. "I have. Quite a lot, actually."

"So what's the problem?"

"That's just it. There is no problem that I can see, except for the very obvious. It's a doozy, so, I'm taking my time."

"Obvious to whom? What the hell are you talking about?"

Only one thing was more uncomfortable for Gwen than talking about her sex life, and that was talking about the glaring disparity between her and Paul. "Despite his love of baseball and horror flicks, his world and mine are in different universes. Remember, right after the anniversary party? We talked about this? You said, if I'm remembering correctly, which I am, that it must be nice to live in the world of plastic surgery and paparazzi, as long as one didn't have many brain cells?"

"That was before I knew him. He's not the airhead I thought he'd be."

"Yeah, I know. But the world he lives in is filled with them. It's a place I have no interest in."

The waitress showed up and they ordered.

Holly shifted in her seat.

It struck Gwen how attractive her friend was. Her curly hair framed her face perfectly, her lips were full and her wide eyes sparked with intelligence and humor. But Gwen would bet a paycheck that no one at The Ivy would look twice at her because she wasn't a traditional beauty.

"Paul doesn't seem to have a problem coming to you. He's loving it. You're exactly what the man needed. Even I can see he looks happier."

"He asked me to go with him tonight, to a dinner at

The Ivy. He was meeting some clients. Show business people. He hated that I said no, but what would I do there? I have nothing in common with those people." And yet, she was jealous. She assumed he'd taken someone else. Someone who fit right in. Someone like Autumn. Or maybe it was Autumn. She shivered.

"What?"

"Nothing." She would not go there. Not ever again.

"You have Paul," Holly said.

It took a moment for Gwen to remember the flow of the conversation.

"You admire his business sense, so there's that. And who knows. He surprised us both. Who's to say we haven't been the ones who have it all wrong? What if there are other terrific, smart, insightful people who just happen to be gorgeous?"

"I don't believe many of them just *happen* to be gorgeous. I think they work very, very hard at it. I know my sisters do." She thought again about Autumn, but refused to dwell. "Good God, it's practically all they can talk about. Working out obsessively, spending all their money on spas and clothes. The only reason they work at all is to finance their addictions."

Holly snorted just as their drinks arrived. She poured her beer, all the while shaking her head. "I'm sorry, but your family can't be representative. I've never met people more obsessed with looks. God, they're impossible."

"That's just it. They are. Between them all, they've injected enough collagen to float a ship."

"Honey, none of them hold a candle to you. You know that, right? Kudos to Paul for being smart enough to see who you are. A man like that isn't to be sneezed at. He clearly wants more in his life than Malibu Barbie."

Gwen wanted to believe it was that simple. "I agree. It's great when he's with us. It won't be like that if I go to his world. They'll all wonder what he's doing with a woman like me. They won't care about what we have in common, or that we have such fun together. They'll judge him, and he won't come out favorably. How can I do that to him? His work is all about keeping up appearances."

"Why do you think he'd give a rat's ass?"

"Even if he doesn't now, he will eventually. He's been that beautiful all his life, Holly. That's what he knows. I just don't think I could stand to watch him be humiliated. It would kill me."

Holly put her hand on Gwen's. "Look, I'm not discounting what you said, or even denying there's some truth in it. Still, I don't think you're giving the man the credit he deserves. You're projecting like mad."

Gwen's first instinct was to dismiss Holly's words. She was a friend and a romantic. Of course she wanted a happy ending. Maybe, though, Gwen was underestimating Paul's strength. She had to admit, he'd surprised her in a hundred ways, why not this?

On the other hand, she'd watched him at the bar, at the ballpark. He used his looks to get what he wanted. It wasn't intentional, rather instinctual. He was used to being fawned over, having the world handed to him on a platter.

Was it possible even with his best intentions to overcome a lifetime of conditioning?

"I know that look," Holly said. "You're thinking too damn much. Here's an idea—what if you just pretend you can't see the future? What if you try to be with him as if it's exactly what both of you should be doing? Let yourself be surprised by what comes next. The worst that can happen is it won't work out. Give it a chance. He deserves that, and so do you."

Gwen tucked into her salad. Could Holly be right? Was she simply projecting her worst fears, and would that cause her to miss out on a chance for real happiness? The hell with the diet. She called over the waitress and ordered a glass of wine.

PAUL WHIPPED OUT the flowers he'd been hiding behind his back. Gwen's mouth opened in a big O that turned into a smile so great it made his whole week better.

"What's this for?" she asked, taking the bouquet of white and rust calla lilies. "They're amazing. How did you know these were my favorite flowers?"

He walked inside feeling pretty awesome. "I didn't. Not for sure, anyway. I knew you liked them because you have that picture in the bathroom."

She kissed him before she shut the door. "Thank you. Come with me into the kitchen so I can put them in water."

He obeyed, happily, thinking he wouldn't mind a cup of coffee. Something that would wake him up. He'd spent all afternoon at Dodger Stadium with a group of producers and directors from the DIY shows he repped. Even though he had three of his people there, it had still been exhausting, and he'd missed most of the game. But the party had gotten them all in one room and they'd agreed to go in together on his year-long promo plans that would cover TV, print and special events.

He'd rather have been alone with Gwen. He'd even have settled for her joining the group, but she'd said she had other things to do.

He sat down on a stool by the bar and watched as she fussed over the flowers. He didn't actually care how they ended up, just that she was happy.

"They're stunning. I love them." She turned to look at him. Her smile faded a bit. "You look exhausted. You want to skip tonight?"

He shook his head. "I've been looking forward to it all day."

She seemed relieved. "Okay. Wine? Beer? Coffee?"

"Coffee would be great."

"Won't take me two seconds." She turned to the cupboard and took out a tiny little coffeemaker, one that made a single cup. She had a little grinder right next to it and in no time the scent of coffee filled the space.

"What else? Did you eat all afternoon, or were you too busy working it?"

"I ate, I think. Nothing too fancy, but really, coffee's all I can handle for the moment. Don't worry, though. After a cup, I'll be ready to go. We can dine anywhere you like."

"Hmm," she said, "I was thinking we might just stay here. Watch a little TV maybe, or I don't know. Perhaps we can find some other way to occupy the evening."

That woke him right up, although he doubted she meant what he hoped she meant. "Here is good. Here is very good."

"I'm glad." She got out some half-and-half, and brought it to him, along with a spoon, a napkin and a white ceramic bowl of sugar.

Paul tried to read her, to see if there was even a remote possibility she'd meant more than watching TV. Her smile was enigmatic, which wasn't unusual. She was always enigmatic.

She'd worn her hair down and soft, begging to be touched. She had on this really silky-looking blouse, light green that went with her eyes. Shit. She was barefoot under her loose-fitting pants. And her toenails were painted, something light and feminine.

She coughed, making him look up at her face. "I can put on shoes if you like."

"No. No, no. I like bare feet. Not that I have a fetish about them or anything. I mean, feet are feet, but it's nice when they look so pretty and... You're laughing at me."

"Yes, I am. In a good way."

He rubbed his face with his hand, thinking it would be really great to take a long, hot shower. Instead, he fixed his cup of coffee and watched her putter. That was enough.

"I had a busy day, myself." Gwen rinsed out the coffeemaker and brewed another cup. "I shopped and got all my veggies together for the week. Very noble. Then I looked for towels and ended up spending a small fortune on tchotchkes I don't need."

"For example?"

"A watering can. Not that they're unnecessary, but I already have a perfectly fine can."

"What enticed you to buy this one?"

She knelt by the cupboard under the sink and took out a funny-looking blue thing that had a long curved spout. "How could I resist?"

"I have no idea. I'm shocked it was still on the shelf."

"Ah, so now you're laughing at me."

"Yes," he repeated. "I am."

"In a good way."

"Always."

"So movies, yes?" she asked. "Shall I make popcorn?"

"Movies, yes. Only make the popcorn if you want it. I guess I ate more at the park than I thought."

"No. We can just veg, and watch anything you like."

"Shall we move to the couch?"

The enigmatic smile returned. "Actually, I was thinking we could watch in my bedroom."

"Bedroom?"

"I have a great TV there."

He was glad he'd put his mug down or he'd have dropped it. He'd been amazingly restrained about the whole sex thing, figuring she'd let him know when it was time. What he didn't know, not for sure, was if this was the signal. Any other woman he'd known, he wouldn't have had to think twice. Gwen was harder to read.

"If you don't want to, the couch is fine."

"No. I'd like to watch TV wherever you're comfortable."

She came over to the bar across from him. "If by watch TV you mean make love, then I'd be comfortable."

He stood. "I can do that. I can do that just fine."

She grinned. "You can finish your coffee."

He smiled back. "I'm done. Great coffee. Seriously, best I've ever had."

She laughed.

He followed her, not ashamed that he kept far enough

back that he could watch her ass the whole way. Now he wished her blouse wasn't so long. Damn, he hadn't considered this was an option. Thankfully, he'd replaced the condom in his wallet. Too bad he hadn't brought two. Funny how he didn't feel tired anymore. He still could use that shower, though.

She led him down a small hallway that had some nice black-and-white pictures on the wall, then to her bedroom. The king-size bed, covered in a purple comforter, was done up girl style with more pillows than he'd ever understand. But nice. There was a major flat-screen TV on the opposite wall, and near the window next to an antique dresser was an armchair and a brass reading lamp.

Then he noticed a champagne bucket set up by the bed. He went to investigate, but there was no actual champagne. Just a couple of Heineken beers and a couple of water bottles in ice. "Hmm," he said, "should I be insulted?"

"Why?"

"You seem pretty confident I was a sure thing."

She came up to him and touched the back of his neck with her hand. Looking into his eyes, her own alight with a mixture of heat and laughter, she nodded. "Reasonably confident," she whispered, just before she kissed him.

They'd kissed a lot since that night on the couch, but this was different. It was a prelude, and that changed everything. Just because he hadn't pushed her didn't mean he hadn't wanted to. It was a whole new thing with Gwen, kind of like reading that damn book. Who knew literary fiction could be foreplay?

He kissed her back, not wanting to go too fast. There was still the shower to deal with before he could let himself splurge.

She pulled back. "What?"

He gave her a sorry look. "How would you feel about me using your shower?"

"I'd feel just fine about it."

"Good. How about now?"

Again, she nodded. "Come on. It's not far."

The bathroom was white and purple, just like her bedroom. Everything looked soft. The towels, the bath mat. She had candles in there, and he could see she used them. Also a big boom box with a stack of CDs next to it. "You like to take baths, eh?"

"My favorite escape."

"Maybe you'd like to escape in the shower with me?"

"I could be persuaded."

He pulled her into his arms. "Please," he said, just before he kissed her, this time with more abandon. Shower sex, with the right accessories, could be a very good thing.

She took her time kissing him back. Before she stopped, her hands reached between them and she started to undo her buttons.

Being a gentleman, he lent a hand, trying to decide if he should stop to watch her strip or just keep on kissing.

Watching won.

He stepped back, working on his own clothes as he witnessed her unveiling. They'd been in such a rush last time that he hadn't taken the time to appreciate her body.

She was slender, but thankfully not as painfully thin

as so many of the women he knew. She even had a little pooch of a tummy that was so sexy he wanted to get down on his knees and kiss it all over.

Her little pussy was trimmed, but not bare, something else that wasn't the fashion, but that, too, appealed to him. Hell, everything about her did.

By the time he'd kicked off his shoes and undone his pants, he was hard. Before he let his jeans go, though, he took out his wallet.

"Wait," she said. "I was a good Scout and bought some of those." Naked and beautiful, she went to one of the drawers where she pulled a packet out of a box. "See?"

"I'll give you your merit badge when we're under the water."

She saluted him, then crossed to the glass-enclosed shower and turned it on. When she looked back, he was ready, his clothes shoved unceremoniously to the side.

She took his hand and they went inside. There was simply no choice, he had to feel her naked and wet. Her body felt amazing, so slick and soft. He explored her with his hands, his eyes, with all the skin he could press against her. She was doing the same thing to him, and it made his cock stiffen further when she grabbed his behind.

After an experiment to see how long they could hold their breaths under the spray, she grabbed the soap and a purple cloth. She built up the lather and then she washed him. It was unreal to just feel her patiently, carefully wash him from his neck to his chest and back. Then she moved down, holding his cock with one hand and using her other hand to bathe him, only for this part the cloth magically vanished and it was skin on skin.

His moan echoed in the shower, and her laugh, as soft as her fingers, swirled around him in the wet. She didn't miss anything, but it was hard to keep still as she left the lower middle section to concentrate on his legs.

He'd really liked that whole lower middle section.

He touched her wet hair as she knelt before him, then it dawned on him that he could do something wonderful for her. He grabbed the shampoo from her silver tray and poured some on his hands before he applied it to her hair.

Knowing how much he loved to be shampooed, he took his time. When she gave up caring if his feet were clean, he drew her up and around, so her back was to him. Since the top of her head reached his chin, it was easy to give her the spa treatment. Now it was her moans and his laughter, and it was all good.

When she was pretty much a damp rag in his arms, he got the spray nozzle and rinsed her so she wouldn't get soap in her eyes. Then he went for the conditioner. Not for her hair so much as for its off-label use. He knew the stuff worked—gentle enough that it wouldn't hurt her. His fingers went down to her pussy, where he took his sweet time getting her ready.

When the moans grew urgent and she had to hang on to him to keep upright, he tore open the condom and slipped it on. Damn thing. He wished he didn't have to use it, but even so, it was more than he could have hoped for.

She kissed his chest and flicked his nipples with the point of her tongue while he adjusted the spray nozzle to hit the side of the shower, high up on the wall. Once his attention returned to her, he licked the moisture off her neck as he steered her toward the warm water spray.

Her gasp told him it was still cold for her up against the glass. Not that she seemed to mind. He took her hands in his, lifting them, pinning them up above her head.

Using his body as a chamois, he rubbed against her, teasing himself with intermittent brushes of his cock against her skin. He wanted this to last, but not enough to stop. She felt too amazing and, Christ, looking at her with the water running down her hair, her ragged breathing as he kept her arms still and high, he whispered, "This is going to be fast and hard. Later is for making love. Now, I want to be inside you so badly I can't…"

It didn't seem to matter that he couldn't find the words.

13

HER NOD WAS SO SMALL he might have missed it if he
hadn't been staring at her with every bit of his attention.
Not at all sure what he'd have done if she objected, he
cast that notion aside as he took her mouth in a kiss
meant to show her just how serious he was.

Her tongue tangled with his as she tried to get the
upper hand, but he was having none of that. He knew
he was being selfish and didn't give a damn. He'd held
off for so long. Thinking about her, going to bed with
only his slick hand for comfort.

He placed her hands together still against the wall.
Holding on to them with one hand, he reached for his
cock. It was raging hard and desperate to be in her.

Without hesitating, with no finesse, only need, he
pushed inside her until he filled her completely. She
cried out, then she kissed him with such ferocity he
knew she wanted more.

Releasing her hands, he lifted her thighs. Gwen
wrapped her legs around his hips, grabbed on to the top
of the shower stall and squeezed his dick.

His head went back as he groaned at the sensation,
but then there was no energy for anything but filling

her, wishing he could disappear inside her, feel this forever.

With their grunts and groans echoing, each time he thrust into her the spray went everywhere. Her legs tightened, one hand went from the wall to his shoulder where she gripped him with bruising strength.

Too soon he started to tremble, to jerk in uneven spasms until he came with a roar in his ears and bright lights behind his lids. This was it, the perfect moment, and he strained and strained until there was nothing left. Even then, he didn't want to move, but had to. There was no strength to hold her.

He let her down gently, moaning as he slipped out.

IT OCCURRED TO GWEN that they should leave the shower, but the task was too daunting. Her heart was pounding, her legs felt like rubber, and she never wanted to move from this spot, from this man.

"You okay?"

She nodded, trying to work up the energy to smile. Screw it. He'd have to take it on faith.

She'd never done it in a shower. Not like this, anyhow. It was just like one of her fantasies, the kind she'd never thought to ask a man to help her play out.

Holly was right. All she'd needed to do was stop thinking. Let herself be with him. He would continue to amaze and delight her, if she only let him.

He turned away after he got the soap, and she washed up a bit before aiming the water in his direction. Motivated, thinking about her bed with him in it, she got out of the shower to grab her towel. He was right behind, and they grinned at each other like kids as they dried off.

With his hair all spiked and his body so stunning it seemed unreal, he nodded toward the other room. They hung up their towels and headed over to the bed, him getting there first to toss pillows in the corner.

As she pulled down the bedding, she wondered what he saw when he looked at her. She knew it had to be pleasurable, but she wondered all the same. Did he see her the way she saw herself? Probably not. When she looked at his face, what she saw was filtered through her life experience, just as hers would be for him. Which confused her, given what his life experience had been. Whoops, that was enough thinking. She'd sworn off it, and she wasn't going to spoil the night by using her pesky brain for anything more taxing than rudimentary speech.

He sighed as he got under the covers, adorably wiggling his feet as he yanked the comforter up his chest. She followed suit, grabbing a cold water on her way. "You want?"

"I think I'll take that Heinie now," he said.

When she stretched to get the bottle, he reached under the covers and pinched her butt.

"Hey!"

"I wasn't talking about beer."

"Oh, that is so lame." She got him his beer, debated touching his chest with the icy bottle, but kindness prevailed. "I expect so much more from you, Mr. Bennet."

"Do you? Bummer. And I was just gonna ask if any of the movies you had in mind were dirty."

She opened her water, sighing as she sat back on the pillows he'd left. "Not a one."

"Damn. So what are our options?"

She listed as many as her poor brain would give her, and he stopped her at *Bull Durham.*

"Really? Excellent. Don't you just love his long-wet-kisses speech? And painting her toenails?"

He had his beer inches from his mouth. "I had no idea you were such a girl. I mean, come on. It's a baseball movie. Yeah, Sarandon's hot, but it's about *baseball*. And just for the record, what's with all the pillows? Don't you have to take them off every single night, and put them all back every single day?"

"Pillows are what define a civilized society. That and the banishment of the designated hitter."

"Wow," he said, lowering his beer. "That was impressive. Pillows and baseball, together. It's all starting to make sense."

"Plebeian. You probably hired someone to decorate your house. A woman, right?"

"No. It was a man. And he wanted to put a pile of pillows on my bed, too, so what does that do to your fancy hypothesis, huh?"

"Actually, it proves it."

Paul looked at her, slowly raising his right eyebrow. "I wish I'd had more to drink. It would have been awesome to belch right now."

She laughed out loud as she shook her head.

The moment, however, was interrupted by a growl from his tummy.

"I need to feed you."

"Don't go," he said. "I'm fine. I'm not hungry."

His stomach protested. Loudly.

She put her water bottle on the nightstand. "I'm going to get snacks. Then I'll put on the movie. You don't have to do anything but think wonderful thoughts."

"You don't want a hand?"

"Nope. I'll be back in a flash." She got out of bed and took her robe from the closet door hook. It was more of a kimono than a robe, and it felt wonderful on her naked skin.

She put together a quick fruit and cheese platter. It wasn't all that miraculous a feat as she'd prepared everything that afternoon. Oh, and she didn't want to forget the chocolate. It had been too expensive and way too many calories, but she'd wanted to take her decadence in one giant swallow. She even grabbed the bottle of champagne from the fridge.

It felt silly, how she'd been too embarrassed to have the champagne in the ice bucket. Another thing she refused to dwell on.

With a full tray, she headed back to the bedroom, anxious about what would happen next. He'd been an animal in the shower. So hot. Remembering made her nipples hard, which was actually pretty neat.

Right before her bedroom door, she paused. She'd barely given herself a moment to relax all day. Because if she'd thought things through, they would have watched the movie on the couch.

She might have been the one who suggested this next step, but there was still so much that made her anxious. Not that she hadn't tried. She'd been vigilant about her thoughts. But he was in her bed. This wasn't a couch quickie. This meant something. It pointed toward a future, and that future couldn't just be him in her world.

Stop it! she told herself. It would all work out. Or it wouldn't. Tonight? *Bull Durham* and sex.

He was on his side, head resting on his hand, watching her as she came into the room.

"Whoa," he said as she put the tray on the bed. "You did all that just now?"

"Of course. We pillow women know our snacks."

"I'm impressed. I'd have had to order out."

She felt a little guilty about the lie. "Want to open the champagne, or should we wait?"

"I'm still working on my beer. Let's put it in ice until we're ready."

She did, and then she got the DVD ready to go. By the time she was back in bed, he was sitting up, eyeing some smoked Gouda.

WHEN THE MOVIE WAS HALF-OVER, the tray was already on the dresser, they each had had some champagne, and Gwen was curled up in the warm cocoon of Paul's arms. She listened more than watched, preferring to toy with the body so conveniently positioned for her pleasure. Her fingers sneaked through his dark hair, curling it, stroking it.

She also played with his nipples, using not just the pads of her fingers but her nails, her lips, her teeth, her breath.

It wasn't clear what he was doing, whether he was glued to the film or awash in sensations. Mostly because she didn't look up. One of his hands was busy, though, rubbing her back, finger-combing her hair, brushing the back of her neck so lightly she shivered.

It made her love *Bull Durham* even more. She'd enjoyed her strawberries and chocolate and her grapes and the Brie. She'd even liked the champagne, which had never been a favorite. It had just seemed right for the occasion. The welcoming of this man into her life. Opening doors she'd kept so firmly closed. Opening herself, at least for the most part.

She hummed a little, the yummy soup song. Because he was.

He lifted the covers from around her shoulders, and she looked up at him. What a lovely sight.

"You do understand what you're doing to me," he asked.

"Hey, I've seen this movie before. I was just killing time until you were finished watching."

He tossed the covers back. "Oh, I'm done," he said, "with everything but you."

"Wow."

On his way down the bed, his very erect penis brushed against her tummy, then her thighs. Her heart started that quick time beat and she forgot how to breathe, but only until she knew he was about to kiss her. Inhaling his strawberry breath, she let him.

This was no against-the-wall kiss. It was slow and deliberate and it made her toes curl. His hand began to stroke her tenderly, caressing her as something precious and beautiful.

The movie hadn't ended, but the sounds became a

wonderful backdrop. Her sheets felt like silk, his skin softer still.

He'd been right. This was making love, and for the first time she allowed herself to think the word. Not just about what he was doing with his tongue and his fingers, but about him. About them.

It made no sense, but maybe love wasn't supposed to. Maybe when the real thing came along it was meant to be crazy, to turn a person's world upside down.

She'd thought it would be one of her weird scientists who would catch her eye and her heart. Someone she'd interview for a job at the Jet Propulsion Laboratory or NASA. It was unbelievable that she was with this man, and that this man had so many of the qualities she had always dreamed of.

He touched her everywhere, teaching her pleasure after pleasure. She held back nothing, loving the feel of every part of him. This dance was slow, erotic, teasing. He stole her breath again and again.

Finally, when it was time, when she was so aroused there were no words for it, he entered her. Slowly. His gaze locked on hers. His need for her as real as the stars. She couldn't look away as he moved inside her. The world had stopped turning, time had paused, and it was just the two of them in all the universe.

Much later, after the movie was over and the lights were off and she was sure he was asleep, she whispered, "I love you," tasting the words, letting herself get used to the sound. It was enough for now.

14

THE FIRST BATCH OF CUPCAKES was in the oven, the red velvet cake making Gwen's kitchen smell like sugar and spice. Holly sat at the bar, impatiently waiting for the frosting to be made so she could sneak a taste.

"I can't believe you're not cranky. I'd be cranky if I hadn't seen my honey since Monday night."

"We've talked. Every day. Sometimes twice a day." Gwen checked to make sure she had all the ingredients out for the frosting. None of that cream cheese stuff for her. This was old-school red velvet frosting. Flour, milk, butter, powdered sugar and vanilla. Every time she made the cupcakes everyone always wanted seconds. It was the only thing her family consistently complimented her on.

"Talking is nice," Holly said. "Boinking is better."

Gwen shook her head. "You need a man, my friend. You need one badly."

"Don't I know it." Holly got up from her stool, came into the kitchen, and went straight to the fridge for a drink. She liked diet cream soda, and Gwen kept it on hand for her, even though she didn't care for it much. Now she also stocked Heineken. Each time she opened the refrigerator door, she thought of Paul.

"I was thinking of trying one of those on-line dating services," Holly said as she put ice in her glass. "I've heard some impressive stories."

"Why not? So many people use them these days. It seems like a good investment."

Holly went back to the bar stool and climbed up. She was in boys gym shorts and an old scrub shirt she'd picked up at a yard sale. Her voluminous hair had been pulled back into a crooked ponytail. She looked great. Why she didn't have someone in her life was a mystery. Holly had it all. Personality, smarts, kindness, compassion. But then, as she'd seen with her own eyes, love was not sensible in the least.

"On the other hand, there are distinct advantages to being single. I could go on a trip at a moment's notice. I can spend my Monday nights at trivia, see every movie I like, even if it's cartoons and eat crackers in bed. Being with someone else means a lot of compromises."

Gwen nodded. "Yeah, all that's true. When you love someone, though, the compromises aren't difficult. Because you want that other person to be happy."

Holly put her glass down on the bar. "Aren't you the woman who wouldn't sleep at Alex's because he kept the thermostat too low? Who refused to go to any Will Ferrell movies, even though he went to see your foreign films?"

"Yes. But we both understood that I was a bitch."

"That's arguable, but let's put that aside for a second. What I want to know is if you've fallen in love with Paul."

"How did we get from Will Ferrell to this?"

"Answer the question, missy!"

Gwen turned her back to hide the smile she couldn't

suppress. She wasn't sure why she'd hesitated to confess all, except that she hadn't told him yet. Not directly. And she had no idea if he felt the same.

"You are. You're in love with him. Holy crap. This is major."

"I didn't say—"

"You didn't have to. How long have we known each other? I can read you like a book, and honey, you've fallen. Does he know?"

She turned back to face Holly. "No. The subject hasn't come up."

"Why not?"

"Because it hasn't. Besides, I'm not even completely sure."

"Hmm, now I always thought love was like pregnancy. Either you are or you aren't."

"That's a fantasy." Gwen checked on the cupcakes, but they had another five minutes to go. "I think love is different for each person. Sometimes it hits with a wallop, sometimes with a touch."

"Which one is it, then?"

Gwen sighed, realizing Holly wasn't going to let it go. Besides, if she couldn't talk about it to her best friend, then what? Left to her own devices, she wouldn't have invited him to her bed. "Both. I can't believe I'm even saying this out loud, but I got it last Saturday night. I realized what I was feeling wasn't a crush, but the real deal. You're right about missing him. It's been hard. The bed feels really empty."

"Do you think he loves you back?" Holly asked, her voice soft and solemn.

"Don't know. Hope so. I know he likes me a lot. That he feels good when he's around me. It's not that simple. Whether I think about them or not, there are still really huge issues. None of that has changed. Look at this week. He's been slammed with work, a different function every night, and I keep dodging him. That can't go on."

"So go with him."

Gwen sighed. "I can't. Not yet. I'm too scared."

"Sweetie, it's not just fun and games anymore. You have your heart at stake. His, too. You're just going to have to step into the arena. Personally, I don't think it's going to be a gigantic issue. But you have to see for yourself."

The timer went off. As Gwen went to the stove, she had to admit her friend was right. Next week, she would do it. Step off the high dive with no guarantee of the landing.

INITIALLY, PAUL THOUGHT the ringing was his phone. He reached for his cell on the nightstand, cursing whatever idiot was calling him on a Sunday morning. When he opened the damn thing, there was no one there. He tossed it on the bed, then lunged for the lamp. Through his wince, he looked at his alarm clock. It was a quarter to ten. That's when he recognized that the ringing was his doorbell.

"Who the hell…" He got out of bed and went downstairs, not bothering to put on any clothes. He wasn't going to let anyone in, so his boxers seemed adequate. The tile floor of his foyer was cold but his anger warmed him.

He'd been up late. After a long night that had kept him in Hollywood at the Kodak theater, he'd come home and picked up yet another book Gwen had challenged him to read, and hadn't gotten to sleep until near three. He'd planned on sleeping late.

He got to the door and looked through the peephole. "Autumn?"

"Come on, sleepyhead. Open the door."

He hadn't seen her since the party at Chateau Marmont, and God, he didn't want to see her now. Groaning, he unlocked the door and let her in.

She kissed him on the cheeks, then took in his attire. "Plaid boxers? I had you pegged for silk or nothing."

"What are you doing here?"

"Is that any way to say good morning on this beautiful day?" She was dressed in low-rise jeans, a skimpy red T-shirt that bared her perfectly flat stomach and sprayed-on tan. Her hair was down around her shoulders, spilling around her beautiful face.

"What are you doing here?"

"I'm stealing you. I know you don't have plans. I spoke to your secretary on Friday, who then peeked at your planner, so don't try to fool me. We're going to a barbecue."

"Autumn—"

She put two fingers to his lips. "I owe you a proper thank-you for rescuing my sister. After the barbecue, I have a big surprise in store, so hurry, hurry. There's no time to lose."

He bit back a sharp reply. He hated Autumn's tone about Gwen and it was a great temptation to tell her he hadn't done the rescuing. In fact, it was the opposite. Instead, he said, "It's too early. You go to the barbecue and call me when you're done."

"Absolutely not. I happen to know you've had a hellish week, that what you need is some real R & R. Don't argue because I won't take no for an answer." She moved back to his front door. "I'm going to wait in the car. Don't be long. We're going to have such a wonderful day."

He opened his mouth to say no, this time more forcefully, but she shut the door in his face. He stared at it, wondering what she would do if he just went back to bed. Eventually, she'd leave, right? She'd get mad, and that would be that. It was a pretty nice solution, but one that probably wouldn't work. If he hadn't met Gwen, he wouldn't have cared, but now he had to end things with Autumn nicely.

Although he'd rather tell her goodbye over a drink, this would have to do. They'd eat their hot dogs or whatever and he'd find a quiet place to end it just before they left. It wouldn't be fun, but these things never were. Actually, with Autumn it shouldn't be that bad. They'd never slept together, and he knew for a fact she saw a lot of guys, so it wasn't as if they'd promised each other a thing. Still, Autumn would pout. She wanted all the boys in the schoolyard to pull her pigtails.

He dragged himself upstairs and climbed into the shower. He'd have liked to linger under the spray, but Autumn had never had much patience. So he got dried, got dressed, brushed everything he was supposed to and headed toward his fate, using the time to practice his speech. How it wasn't her, it was him. Complimenting her greatly on her beauty and personality. It would end eventually, and then he could come back home and take a nap.

As he climbed in next to her, he asked, "What's all

that?" nodding toward the package and basket in the backseat.

"Stuff for the barbecue." She drove the way she got through life, as if the road belonged to her alone and anyone in her path should have known better. It seemed unreal that he'd wanted her so badly. Like someone else's life. It said, he supposed, a lot about his values. His old values. "Where are we going?" he asked, more anxious than ever to get this over with.

She turned to him, ignoring the road and all the other cars. He put his hand on the dashboard and his foot on his imaginary brake and hoped his death would be swift. Finally, she paid attention to driving again. "I'm not going to tell you. You need some surprises in your life. Let this be the first of many. I've got a whole bunch planned for us today."

"I don't like surprises."

"Everyone likes surprises."

"Autumn, I mean it—watch out, that light's red."

She laughed as they crossed the intersection to the sound of horns honking and people cursing, his own choice words joining the chorus.

How on earth had Gwen and Autumn come from the same parents?

CONSIDERING THE SIZE of Gwen's family, it was odd that there were only two in her parents' kitchen. Next to her, working on the deviled egg platter, was Virginia, the housekeeper, who'd been with the family since Gwen was a kid.

It was past eleven. The invitation had been for ten,

but most of her clan liked to make entrances, so it was a staggered business.

Her father was with her brother-in-law, Harry, one of the birthday girl's parents. They were preparing the barbecue grill, although she couldn't imagine why there was such a big discussion. It wasn't as if they had to light anything. The behemoth gas grill was part of their outdoor kitchen, the one her mother had designed after watching a lethal dose of home improvement shows. There was a brick pizza oven, a fridge, a wine cooler, an oven, even a rotisserie. Everything was done in stainless steel and granite, and her parents used it probably twice a year.

Well, it didn't matter. It was their fun, their home. They seemed happy, and she hoped it was so.

A couple of the kids were in the pool, splashing under the waterfall, while their parents sipped their Bloody Marys. Gwen couldn't see them, but she heard most everything. The splashing, the loud exclamations of how great everyone looked, and how amazing it was that Nickie was one already.

It was nice. For the first time in ages, none of them could get to her. All she had to do was step back and wish them well. It was no skin off her nose if they wanted to spend all their time obsessing over clothes and skin care. In fact, she hoped all of them were delighted with their families and their jobs.

"Those cupcakes look great, Gwen." Virginia shifted one of the decorated treats on the three-tiered platter. "I made my niece one of your red velvets for her graduation. Everyone loved it."

"I'm glad. I can never make it unless I'm going somewhere. If I had them in my kitchen, I'd eat every one all by myself."

"Is that Autumn?"

Gwen listened, and yep, there was her sister's laugh wafting in from the front door. "I haven't seen her in a while."

"She doesn't come by here much. She spends so much time out of the country now. Your mom worries."

"I doubt she'll be flying much longer. It's about time for her to pick one of her fabulous men and settle down."

"I hope she gets someone who'll treat her well. She can pick some doozies."

Gwen smiled. "Every once in a while, someone fabulous sneaks through."

Virginia shrugged. "That had to be when I was on vacation. Anyway, I'm gonna take this first batch of appetizers out there. How about you work on the salad?"

"No problem." Gwen got out the big cutting board and rinsed the chef's knife, ready to chop a mound of fresh veggies, feeling quite snug in the kitchen.

There was Autumn's voice again, although Gwen couldn't make out the words. Just the familiar singsong lilt. Gwen had considered asking Paul to this shindig, but decided his week had been hellish enough. What he needed today was to rest.

The temptation had been strong, though. Not just to have his company, but to be there when Autumn arrived. To see her face when the guy she'd bribed to take pity on her ugly sister was on that ugly sister's arm. She would have hit the roof.

Every one of her siblings would be stunned beyond belief if they knew. Part of her wanted to tell them all, but she wouldn't. Things were just beginning with her and Paul, and it was still a private matter. Well, except for Holly.

With any luck, Gwen would get out of here early, Paul would have caught up on his sleep, and she'd see him tonight.

The thought made her shiver in anticipation. It had been too long with just his voice. She wanted him to spend the night. To make love to him, to tease him. To wake up with him beside her.

Who would have guessed in a million years she would be so happy with one of Autumn's gorgeous guys? She'd definitely keep her secret. She didn't want anything to spoil her bliss.

PAUL DIDN'T KNOW what the hell to do. At first, he hadn't immediately made the connection. It had slowly dawned on him, after walking through the house to the backyard, exactly where he was. If he'd had any idea Autumn was going to drag him to a family affair, he'd never have agreed. Of course, Autumn suspected as much, but why would she care what he wanted?

He hadn't seen Gwen. No one had brought up her name. Why hadn't he known about this party? Gwen hadn't mentioned it, which seemed odd. Unless she hadn't come. Yeah, that sounded right. She hadn't said anything because she'd blown it off. Still, he'd rather have been anywhere else.

Autumn was hanging all over him, showing him off

like a prize pony. Most of her family remembered him, and although no one said anything, he sensed they were all relieved to see him with whom they considered the right sister.

What he wanted was to get the hell out of there. Goddamn Autumn. This was insane. All he'd wanted to do was end whatever nonsense they'd had. They'd barely spoken since their last awkward date. She'd sent that tacky Venus for some unknown reason, then left him text messages wondering why he wasn't calling her. The two times he'd left voice mail for her, she'd ignored him.

Until this.

"You're in public relations, isn't that right?"

Paul nodded at Mark, one of the brothers-in-law. His wife, Eve, had asked what he'd like to drink, and although he could have used a shot of whiskey for fortification, he'd declined, wanting to make his exit as simple as possible. He'd call a cab, that's all. The question was, should he just leave, making up some story, or tell Autumn he was seeing Gwen? Damn. Everything was more awkward now, and while he knew it was important to set the record straight, he didn't want to embarrass her unnecessarily.

"I've used a few PR firms," Mark said, leading him farther out in the large yard. "I'm in real estate. Commercial, not residential. Mostly, I build shopping centers, the small ones. Doesn't matter what the home market is, everybody needs someplace to buy coffee and tampons." He laughed at his joke with a sound that Paul remembered from the party. It had been so loud he'd heard it while the band was at full volume.

Although he was pretty damn sure Gwen wasn't here, he looked around for her, just in case. Thankfully, he didn't see her. With her dislike of her family, she'd undoubtedly made up some excuse. He prayed he was right.

"Come on, sweetie, don't you want a drink? My brother makes a wicked Bloody Mary. Complete with hot sauce and celery stick. I know you'll love it." Autumn touched his arm and fluttered her eyelashes.

"I don't care for tomato juice," he said, and not for the first time. Gwen knew that about him. She knew a lot more than that, more than maybe anyone ever had. "Is there somewhere we can talk?"

"Sure. Give me a minute, okay? I haven't seen the birthday girl, and I want to show you off to Bethany and Faith."

Paul figured it might be best to wait until she had her drink in hand before he spilled the beans. Let her have a minute to say her hellos before he called himself on his cell. He'd learned that trick from a model he'd dated. It was sneaky, but by dialing a certain sequence of numbers, he could make his own phone ring.

He walked with Autumn to the outdoor kitchen space, large by any standard, and tried to keep things polite but distant. It became more and more bewildering that Gwen was a part of this family. All he needed were a couple of cameras for the perfect family TV commercial. They all were exceptionally attractive, even the kids. They all knew just what to wear, how to hold themselves, what shade of hair would catch the light. Autumn was the prettiest of the bunch, but not by much. And wasn't it interesting that he found her beauty so incredibly empty?

He much preferred Gwen's honest, lovely face. All the things he'd have ignored such a short time ago captivated him now. She was just so much more. More than surface looks. More than games. More than even sex. It was the depth of her that had gotten to him. Which was nuts. He was the last person on earth who should have seen that.

"You two are a picture." Autumn's mother smiled as if it were her daughter's wedding. "In fact, Frank? Get the camera. I want to preserve this moment on film."

"Really, don't bother," Paul said. "Honestly, I hate taking pictures."

"That's such a lie, you big goof." Autumn grabbed his hand as she took her drink from her brother. "You love to be in the limelight. I just can't believe you haven't capitalized on your looks. You could have been a movie star."

"Except for the fact that I can't act, I'm sure you're right."

Autumn's laugh sounded flat and fake, yet he'd been entranced by it before. He needed to tell her, and leave.

"Look this way, you two."

Paul couldn't think how to get out of it. So he smiled as she snuggled closer. Gave it his PR best.

Five more minutes, then he'd get her inside.

GWEN STOOD by the open sliding-glass door holding a plate of smoked salmon and mini bagels. She didn't feel the warm breeze or hear the children splashing in the pool. Her gaze was on Paul as he posed for a picture, Autumn draping herself over him like a pampered cat.

It had all been a joke. A trick. It meant nothing. Of

course. What had made her think, even for a second, that Paul could love her? That he would choose *her?*

She turned slowly, needing to put the platter down. Needing to find her purse, get out her keys.

Behind her, she heard his voice calling her name.

She had to get out before she heard that voice ever again. Before he could see that he'd broken her.

15

"GWEN, WAIT!" Paul dislodged Autumn's arm and ran toward the house. He almost tripped over a small child, who got freaked out despite the fact that he hadn't touched her. Even though he told her she was fine, she howled, and then a whole herd of people came charging. Finally he managed to make his way inside, just in time to see the front door close.

He made a mad dash for the door as he ran to catch Gwen. She was already in the car, the door slamming when he reached her. He banged on the hood. "Wait. I can explain."

She looked at him as if she'd never seen him before, then she turned on the engine and took off. He followed her into the street even though he knew it was useless. He watched her until the car disappeared around the corner, cursing his luck.

"Paul?"

He turned to see Autumn on the front grass, her drink still in her hand, her perfect face marred by signs of confusion. "What's going on?"

He threw up his hand in the general direction of Gwen's car, then realized he couldn't just go. Autumn deserved an explanation. Not that his behavior made it easy. "I was going to tell you," he said, walking toward her, dreading each step. "I wish we'd had a few private moments before all this, just so I could explain."

"What were you doing running after Gwen?"

The way she said her sister's name made things easier. "We've been seeing each other."

Autumn stared at him, her mouth open. "Why?"

"Because I like her. In fact, I think it's more than that."

Her mouth opened wider; instead of just confusion there was a little panic in her eyes. Then she laughed. "Oh, wow. For a minute there, I thought you were serious. Jeez, what a dope I am. Come on, let's get back to the party."

He put his hand on her arm. "I'm not joking. I should have told you before this, but we never did seem to connect. I'm very fond of Gwen, and if she doesn't hate me for today, I think she feels the same. At least, I hope so."

"Now you're just freaking me out. Stop it. I don't think it's very nice of you. Gwen can't help how she looks."

"Autumn, I know you don't know me well. All we ever did was flirt. I'm completely serious. In fact, I need to go after her." He pulled out his cell phone and flipped it open.

Autumn took a step closer, then another. And slapped him. Hard across the cheek. Just like in the movies, only it hurt like a mother.

"You prick. You like her? You want Gwen? That's just wrong. It makes me ill to think of you— If you wanted to stop seeing me, you could have come up with a better excuse."

"Jesus, Autumn. Whatever you think of me, she's still your sister."

"I can't believe I was going to sleep with you today," she said, her voice low.

She turned, walked a few steps, then turned again. "She's not going to fuck you, you know. Not Miss Superiority. Miss Perfect. She doesn't believe in sex without love."

"Not an issue." He dialed information and listened for the ring.

Autumn nearly dropped her drink. Her anger reddened her cheeks and actually made her look very pretty. Too bad there wasn't a Truth in Advertising law for people.

Actually, that wasn't true. If there had been, Gwen wouldn't have looked at him twice. Now, he just needed to get to her. Once she heard what had happened, she'd understand. After all, she was Gwen.

THE DRIVE HOME had been a blur. No tears, just an odd combination of numbness and a pain that was as physical as a blow to the chest.

He'd looked so natural with her family. On Autumn's arm. It made such sense. It was the smile that had done it. Made her see what a fool she'd been.

She'd loved him. Still must if it hurt so badly to see the truth. She'd finally let down her defenses. She'd actually dreamed of a future together, a shared life.

The humiliation was almost as painful as the heartbreak.

She dropped onto her couch, staring at nothing, feeling shattered. How could she have been so stupid?

Even though she knew it was warm in her apartment, she felt chilled to the bone. The throw was just there, on the other side of the couch but she couldn't make herself get it. Everything was out of reach. Comfort, warmth. Love.

She'd have to tell Holly. The thought of her friend's pity made Gwen sick to her stomach. She'd leave, just go somewhere no one knew her. Were they all laughing at her, back at the party? Having themselves a good chuckle as they ate her red velvet cupcakes?

Someone banged on her door. She made herself get up, to walk, to open.

It was Paul.

"Go away," she said, shutting the door.

He wedged his foot inside. "No. It wasn't what it looked like."

"Just leave," she said, not wanting him to see the tears in her eyes.

He pushed his way inside. "Gwen, listen to me. I had no idea she was taking me to a family gathering. The only reason I was with her was because I needed to tell her about us. It wasn't fair to spring it on her, that's all. That's what happened anyway. It wasn't intentional. I've hardly spoken to her since we hooked up, and I thought it would be better to lay it all out in person. I wouldn't hurt you for the world. I didn't want to hurt her, either. Now, I've done both, but I didn't mean to."

The words trickled slowly into her brain. After what seemed like a lifetime, she understood two things: he was telling the truth and that the truth didn't matter.

He stepped toward her, reaching out to touch her arm.

She stared at his hand. "I believe you."

"So everything's okay?" he asked, but his voice showed he didn't think it was.

"Yes. It's okay. I get it now. I like you, Paul, and I know you like me. That doesn't change things though, does it?"

"What things?"

"The fact that you and I aren't meant to be together. We never have been. You belong with someone like Autumn. Hopefully someone nicer, but like her. Someone you can take to your parties and your premieres. We're just too different."

"I've invited you over and over. I want you with me."

She studied his face, incredibly aware of his stunning looks. No matter what his intentions were, she'd never feel truly comfortable with him in his world. "I don't want to go there with you. I'm sorry, but it's the truth."

He inhaled sharply, looking stricken. "Okay. Fine. I won't ask you. I can do all that crap on my own."

She hugged herself, so very cold. "No. It's not a minor deal. And it's not just about parties. I hate that it's true because I've lived so much of my life believing that this shouldn't matter. I'd convinced myself that I was fine about my looks and that I didn't care about anyone else's opinion. I'm the shallow one. Not you. You're fine. You're terrific. But I couldn't take the stares. All of them wondering what you're doing with someone like me."

"You underestimate yourself."

She turned away from him, deeply ashamed, but unwilling to lie about it. "I thought I was someone else. Someone better. I'm not."

"Look, let's sit down. Talk about this. I don't even understand where this is coming from. Please."

Shattered, she shook her head. She didn't want to cry, but the tears came. "No. I'm sorry. I admire you so much. I know you'll meet someone just right. You'll see it makes sense." She went to the door. "Please, just go."

"Gwen, let me stay."

She closed her eyes, the sight of him hurting too much.

Finally, he left. And she let herself weep. For the loss of him, and for the truth about herself.

PAUL WAS STILL UP after midnight. He'd called her twice, but she hadn't picked up. He'd made every argument in his head, why she was wrong, why they made perfect sense together. But the longer he argued, the more her words sank in.

He thought about his business. His clients may not be the highest class out there, but they were all his kind. The kind he'd always associated with. And they were nothing compared to his friends.

To a man, and most especially to a woman, each was the type to judge everyone and everything on the superficial. In other words, they were just like him.

He still didn't fully understand what had drawn him to Gwen. Was it that she presented a challenge? From the get-go, she hadn't been impressed with his looks, the company he kept, his success, his money. He'd been surprised that night at the party that he'd enjoyed being with her. He'd assumed she'd be dry and dull, that they'd have nothing in common.

Well, that had been true to some degree. Yes, they

both were baseball fans, and she loved Japanese horror, but those were coincidences.

He went to the kitchen and took out his decanter of whiskey. He needed something to put him to sleep.

He poured a double, neat, and swallowed the damn thing in one gulp. It burned his throat, made him cough.

When he went back to his study, he looked at the bookshelves. They were built-ins, and there were lots of hardbacks in neat rows—the majority still unread. Hers had been the first novel he'd read in years.

Then he thought about the books shelved in her living room. Novels, history, philosophy, film criticism. He knew without doubt that she'd read them all.

What would she want with a guy like him? She'd seen through his bullshit. She knew he was a show dog.

He sat down in his expensive leather chair. He'd had fun with Gwen. Monday night trivia had turned into something he looked forward to. He wanted to play on her team, go with her to the movies. Making love with her had been amazing.

Even so, he had to admit there was a chasm. If he was honest with himself, it would have bothered him in the end. His friends would look down on her. She wouldn't fit in with his clients or associates. She'd see them for who they really were, and then he'd have to make some hard choices.

The facades had been enough all his life. It was easier that way. He understood those rules, and in that game he was an unqualified winner.

Did he really want to rock the boat?

Gwen was a challenge. She'd always be a challenge.

It had started to feel as if he could win her, too, but maybe she was right. In the long run, wouldn't it get old, always trying to be someone he wasn't? To keep up with her would mean seeing the world through different eyes. Frankly, he had no idea if he'd be up to the task.

He didn't want her to be right. When he'd told Autumn he liked Gwen, maybe more than that, he'd told the absolute truth.

What he hadn't considered was the future. Gwen deserved the best man in the world. He didn't come close.

GWEN CALLED IN SICK for the first time in almost a year. From bed she'd turned on the television with the remote, but she couldn't say what was on.

Her eyes burned from crying; that was nothing compared to the pain in her heart. There was no reasoning with herself. She knew she'd done the right thing. It had already gone too far, and if it hurt this badly now, what would it be like months, years from now when they both realized how they were a complete mismatch?

She could just picture the two of them walking into Mr. Chow or Nobu. The looks of disbelief on all those perfect faces. They'd assume she was his sister or client or someone he had to dine with.

She couldn't, wouldn't do that to Paul. Or herself.

The phone rang again and she let the machine pick it up. It was Holly for the fourth time. Gwen should have answered, but couldn't. Holly would understand, still, she'd want to talk about it. No.

It was all such a damn shame. She got another tissue out of the almost-empty box and blew her nose. She'd been so happy. Deliriously. She had to laugh at that. Delirious was right. She'd been swept up in a fairy tale. It was smart to have put an end to it.

If only she could sleep for a few months. Wake up with no memory of loving him.

But she'd live. And one day, she probably would click with one of her scientists. It helped that Paul hadn't called in a while. She hoped he never would.

Curling around her pillow, she remembered his scent, his laughter, the way she'd felt when he touched the small of her back.

The sobs started and they stayed throughout the night.

16

"IT'S MS. CHRISTOPHER, on line two."

Paul's heart sped up, his breathing quickened and he picked up the phone so fast he knocked over a stack of files. "Gwen?"

Silence. Finally, "No. Autumn."

Everything in him deflated like a flat tire. It had been almost a month since he'd last seen Gwen or spoken to Autumn. He felt like hanging up the phone without a word, but if there was even a slim chance that Autumn had news about her sister, he'd stick with it. "Sorry. Hi, Autumn. What can I do for you?"

"You could try and be a little happier to hear from me."

"You sound good," he said, knowing the compliment would soothe her ego.

"I would be, if I wasn't missing you so much. I know we said some things we both regret. That's a pity because we used to get along so well."

"We did." That was before Gwen, of course, but it was true nonetheless.

"So how about we go out to dinner? My treat. Wherever you want. Whenever. I'm here for a week, so I can clear my book. I'd like to apologize. Seriously. It doesn't have to be anything more than that. I just feel so bad."

It was Monday, and Mondays weren't easy for him, still. He kept thinking about baseball trivia. About the great wings and hot sauce. Holly and the rest of the gang. He missed everything about Monday night.

"Paul?"

"Yeah, sorry. I appreciate the offer, but I don't think so. Besides, I can't imagine you don't have a dozen men right now that would love nothing more than to be with you."

"Oh, honey," she said, her voice as he remembered from before. Breathy, feminine, beguiling. She was turning it on for his benefit, although he couldn't fathom why.

Then it occurred to him. The first clue he'd had about Autumn had come from Gwen. She'd told him that the trick to sleeping with Autumn was to not want her. He smiled as he recalled her exact words: "...then her legs will part like the Red Sea."

Why wasn't he surprised that Gwen had been exactly right?

"I've got a meeting to get to, Autumn. Thanks for the call and the invitation. We're not meant to be, that's all. I wish you well."

"That's it?" Gone was the flirtation, the cajoling lilt. "I know you're not seeing her anymore. And we never—"

"I've got to run. Take care of yourself. Let someone else drive."

"But—"

"Goodbye." No, he wasn't seeing Gwen anymore. Just thinking about her every day. Every night.

He'd worked hard to convince himself that it was for the best. That he and Gwen would never have made it.

That might have even been true, if he could have gone back to being his old self.

She'd ruined it. Or he'd ruined things for himself. He'd changed in ways that constantly caught him off guard. He used to love going to the ballpark, but it had lost its magic. He still went, still cheered for his team. And he thought about Gwen.

He'd had some dates. He'd tried to hook up with the kind of woman he'd always been attracted to. Gorgeous, connected. Actresses and models. Maybe he'd just found particularly dull companions. In any event, there were none he wanted to pursue. Then he'd tried going against type, but it was soon clear that he could find women who had one or two traits that reminded him of Gwen, but none of them had the whole package. Jennifer had made him hope, because she'd looked a little like Gwen, but she'd been self-conscious the whole evening, barely saying a word.

It sucked. The whole thing.

He'd continued reading. Many a night he'd fallen asleep with some big hardback on his chest. But there was no one to discuss it with.

Damn, she'd even tainted poker night. His friends weren't as funny, cared about things that no longer interested him. They all assured him he'd snap out of it. He wasn't so certain.

He picked up the phone. Stared at it for a while, wondering yet again if she'd answer. Or if she'd just tell him to leave her alone. In the end, he put it down and went back to signing checks, wondering what she was doing.

SOMEONE NAMED YoMama was ahead of Gwen by ten points. She had no idea who he was and worse, she didn't care. She'd been dethroned almost a month ago, after she'd returned to trivia night at Bats and Balls. Her friends continued to be concerned about her, which was very nice, but she wished they'd all stop looking at her as if she'd been in some horrible accident. She hadn't lost a limb. Just a man. A man who continued to haunt her.

"You want another one?"

She shook her head at Holly. Gwen didn't want another beer or wings or popcorn or cheering up or anything else. Her only wish was for the pain to stop. She'd known it would be difficult, but good God she'd been unprepared for just how painful it would be.

She felt as if she were living some sort of half life. That she was back in black-and-white Kansas after the dazzle of Oz. Her job was something to get through. Hell, everything was something to get through. One step, then another. No respite even in sleep, as he came to her night after night in her dreams.

The worst of it was how her mind insisted on tormenting her with scenarios in which the two of them had made it. Got engaged, got married, moved to Europe, joined a cult, anything that ignored the truth.

Holly, bless her, had finally stopped urging her to try again with Paul. Even her best friend couldn't take away the ache, no matter how much she tried.

Gwen looked up just in time to see she'd missed another question. Why did she even bother coming?

Mondays were difficult enough without showing up at the bar. Holly had sworn that getting back into the swing of her life would help, but it hadn't. Nothing helped. She could barely watch the Dodgers play. She hadn't gone to movies, had excused herself from softball knowing that she'd be no use.

"Hey, would you pay attention?" Holly said. "Even I know the answer to that one."

Gwen looked up at the big screen and hit the correct button on her machine. "Thanks," she said, working to sound cheerful.

"I meant to tell you, there's a film festival coming to Century City next week. We can get a pass for about fifty bucks. Want to?"

She didn't. She also didn't want to shut Holly out yet again. "Let me see what the movies are. I'll let you know tomorrow."

"Sure, that'd be great." Holly's words were upbeat, hopeful, but her tone was filled with concern.

Gwen smiled at her friend, wishing it could be different. She made herself participate in the game until the last question had been asked, and the winners listed. She was in the top twenty-five. She tried to care.

The drive home was quiet, as it always was these days. Holly parked and said good-night. The moment Gwen was alone, the prospect of the long night ahead filled her with dread.

Someone was at her front door, but she could see it wasn't him. It was a woman. The closer she got in the hallway, the slower her steps grew as she realized it was Autumn.

What the hell was she doing there? Gwen thought about turning around, getting into her car and just driving until she was sure Autumn had left. But then her sister called out her name and it was too late.

"What are you doing here?" Gwen asked, not even attempting to disguise how much she didn't want Autumn there.

"I need to talk to you."

"About what?"

Autumn, her makeup perfect, her outfit perfect, scowled. "Just open the damn door."

Regretting it even as she put her key in the lock, she let Autumn in, then followed. The apartment was messy. The newspaper and her morning coffee were still on the table. She'd left dishes in the sink and her sweater from two nights ago remained draped over the couch.

Once the lights were on, she wished for the darkness. For Autumn to go away. Seeing her made everything worse. "Say what you came to say."

Full of righteous indignation Autumn glared at her as she had since childhood. "I want to know what you said to him."

Gwen put down her purse. "What?"

"What did you tell him about me?"

"I didn't tell anyone anything."

"Don't play coy with me, Gwen."

The sound of her name on Autumn's lips made Gwen wince. There was such ugliness to her sister, more and more the older she got. "I have no patience for your histrionics, Autumn. If you have a point, get to it."

"Paul doesn't even want to talk to me anymore."

Gwen's stomach twisted and her throat wanted to close, but she held on, not giving a thing away. "That's his choice. I had nothing to do with it."

"You had to. He was falling for me. He used to call me all the time, begging to see me." She paced a bit in her high heels. Why anyone would wear stilettos with jeans was beyond Gwen. But then, she didn't understand anything about her family.

"He used to call me when I was in Rome. He sent me presents. He wanted me, and you did something to him. You tricked him. That's the only reason a man like Paul would have anything to do with you."

"Get over yourself, if that's even possible. You only want Paul because he doesn't want you. Well, tough. Deal with it. Just leave me the hell alone. Go home."

"You don't know the first thing about me."

"That's right." Gwen went to her couch, but thought better about sitting down. She had the feeling she might need to physically show Autumn the door. "I don't want to know anything about you. I haven't got the five minutes to spare."

"What five minutes? What are you talking about?"

"Never mind. Whatever your problems are, they've got nothing to do with me. I haven't spoken to Paul since the party. Satisfied?"

"No. Whatever you did, you need to fix it. He's horrible now. Everyone we know thinks he's sick. In the head, okay? He's got some kind of screw loose, and you did that to him."

Gwen felt something she hadn't in a long time. She shouldn't be glad Paul was miserable, but there it was.

Naturally, she wasn't going to let Autumn see that, either. "Can't help you. I have no interest in Paul Bennet. No idea what he's doing. If you're smart, you'll let it go, too."

"I always knew you were weird, but I never thought you'd be this selfish. Even Faith thought you'd be willing to help. Wait till I tell her what a bitch you're being."

"Tell Faith whatever you like. Now get out. I mean it. The discussion is over."

"I hope you get what you deserve," Autumn said as she marched to the door.

"Same back atya," Gwen whispered as she locked up.

Everyone thought Paul was sick? In the head? Funny, pretty much everyone she knew thought the same thing was wrong with her. Only her friends were observant enough to know that she was suffering from heartbreak.

It was unthinkable to her "loving" family that Paul could have been attracted to her for being her.

How could she blame them, though, when it was still mostly unthinkable to her?

He'd been so much of what she wanted in a significant other. And yet, unless she was able to picture them living a real life, it was no good at all, was it?

She headed for the bedroom and flopped onto the bed. This was ridiculous. She simply couldn't go on this way. Something had to be done, something drastic.

Why on earth did she still allow her family to get to her? Why was she even here? Just because she always had been? Pasadena was great, but it wasn't the only place. She'd always wondered about living in Chicago or New York. Rockland-Stewart had offices all over the country. There was nothing preventing her from putting in for a transfer.

Yes, it would mean leaving her friends. That would be hard, especially leaving Holly. What would she do without Holly to turn to?

Wait. There were telephones, the Internet. Airplanes. They could still be in touch, as much as ever. It would be different, but different didn't mean bad.

In fact, the more she thought about it, the more she liked it. She'd move, somewhere she didn't know a soul. No suburbs for her, either. She was a city girl and she wanted the liveliness and adventure a big city offered. It would take a long time to discover a new town, a new state. Why the hell not?

Then she wouldn't have to make excuses for not going to family gatherings. Everyone would be relieved. She'd miss watching her nieces and nephews grow up, but hey, once a year, maybe at Christmas? That would be plenty.

She'd be so busy in her new life she wouldn't have time to think about Paul. It was a brilliant solution. She'd find a book club, a sports bar, and while she'd never stop loving her Dodgers, she'd find other teams to root for, too.

With more enthusiasm than she'd had for over a month, she went to the bathroom to get ready for bed. There would be a million things to do to get ready. A transfer depended on openings in the company, but she knew they'd work hard to place her. Then there'd be housing to look for. She'd been saving for a house for a hell of a long time, so she'd be able to make a substantial down payment. No, the finances wouldn't stop her.

Nothing would.

Thousands of miles away, she wouldn't wish for every call to be from him. She'd stop looking for him in crowds. Monday nights wouldn't be torture, and she'd learn to love baseball with her old joie de vivre.

If she was lucky, she'd quit dreaming about him. It seemed too much to hope for, but then she was still here. At the scene of the crime.

After her T-shirt was on, her face washed, her lotion slathered on, she returned to the bedroom. The sheets from that night were in the back of her linen closet. Even those towels had been stowed away. How foolish was that? They were things. Of no particular significance except what she bestowed upon them. It was childish beyond words to not want to wash her face with the same washcloth.

She crawled under the covers. First thing, she turned on the TV. There was no chance of falling asleep without it. She needed just enough noise to distract her. In the car, in the office, but especially here.

Then she shut off the lights and started a list of all the things she'd have to do to move across the country.

That worked for about ten minutes, and then he came back. Paul, touching her. How he kissed, and how it felt to lick him like a sinful treat.

She turned over, determined to go on with her list. Determined but weak.

It was later than usual before she wept, so she was thankful for that. God, how she missed him. So much, it hurt to breathe.

Her thoughts skittered from one memory to another

and landed on that first night. She remembered him at her door, so handsome in his tuxedo. The first dance. How shocked she'd been that he'd been so good. They'd laughed a lot that night. Yeah, they'd also had a lot to drink, but that wasn't it. That wasn't the important thing. They'd had a wonderful time in a place where she'd never expected it.

Yes, it had been more his world than hers, despite the fact that it was her family and he hadn't known anyone. She hadn't cared what anyone in the room thought.

What had happened to her? Where had she lost that confidence? Where had she lost *herself?*

She'd spent years as a self-confident, proud woman. Someone of substance. It made no sense that she'd lost something she'd believed to be so fundamental.

Was it possible to find that Gwen again?

She wasn't much into prayer. She'd always been too logical for that kind of thing. Logic be damned. She needed all the help she could get if she were to have any hope of finding her truth.

"Please, God," she whispered, "if you're there, help me. Let me be me again. I miss myself almost as much as I miss Paul, and I don't know how to fix it."

17

"I CAN'T DO THIS." Gwen put her hairbrush down and looked at Holly, who stood next to Gwen's bed, a bag of chips in her lap, a soda on the nightstand at the ready.

"Don't be silly. Of course you can. It's only a date."

"A blind date. What was I thinking? I'm not ready."

"Gwen Christopher," Holly said in schoolmarm mode. "It's been two months. You have nothing whatsoever to do tonight except watch TV, and there's nothing good on. Would you, for pity's sake, consider the possibility that you could have a good time tonight?"

"I don't know this man. Even if he was Mr. Wonderful, I'm in no mood. I've been dreading this since I let you talk me into it. Call him and tell him something came up. Say I had to fly to Yemen."

"I will not. You're going to go, and dammit, you're going to have a good time."

"Ha." Gwen looked at herself in the mirror. Holly had told her it was just a movie, jeans were fine, nothing to worry about. Gwen wasn't even sure why she'd bothered with makeup. The whole business was a bad idea. All she could think about was Paul. Which wasn't fair. She turned to Holly. "Why would you want to inflict me on a perfectly innocent stranger? What did he ever do to you?"

"Very amusing." Holly's words were garbled by chips, but Gwen understood. "Wait till you meet him. You'll relax instantly, and before you know it you'll be laughing and all thoughts of your tragic life will vanish."

"Impossible."

Her friend put down the bag. "Won't you please, please trust me? I know how hard it's been for you. At some point you have to move forward. It's time, my friend. Past time."

Gwen sighed. Holly was wrong. Missing Paul had only gotten worse as each day passed. She'd tried to call him so many times, but fear had won out in the beginning and by the time the fear had lessened, awkwardness swooped in to take its place. There was little doubt he'd moved on. Surely he had a woman in his life. Someone more appropriate. Someone who didn't have to struggle with old neuroses.

"I know what you're thinking. Being with Paul brought up some past demons. It happens. You faced them, and now you're stronger. You're you again, with no apologies. Which makes it perfectly sensible that it's time for you to get out there. Meet someone. I promise, he's terrific."

Gwen crossed her arms. "Then why aren't you going out with him?"

Holly made a face. "He's too smart for me."

"Hey, cut that out. You're everything a man could want. I wish you wouldn't say things like that about yourself."

"Said the kettle."

After a short but sweet raspberry, Gwen went to her closet and pulled out her white jacket. It seemed to go with her dark jeans and navy striped top. Although it didn't make a damn bit of difference what she wore, seeing as how she didn't want to go, and wouldn't have a good time.

"You'd better get a move on." Holly swung her legs over the side of the bed, the chip bag still open in her left hand.

"I'll be early."

"Only if you don't hit traffic. Which you will."

"Did you tell him it was only for the movie? No dinner afterward or anything like that?"

"I did not." Holly wiped her free hand on her sweats and came over to Gwen. "Just see what happens. You'll have your own car, right? If it sucks you can leave after the movie. How bad could it be?"

"Bad." Gwen put the jacket on as she gave in. It was only a movie. She'd survive. And then maybe Holly would stop trying to fix her up. She knew her friend meant well. From Holly's perspective it must look as if Gwen's life was back on track. She was winning at trivia again, doing things with the gang from work. She'd even remembered how to laugh. It hadn't been easy, but she'd been determined to find herself. To make sure that while she may have lost Paul, she would never go back to that place of doubt.

If he somehow miraculously walked back into her life, she wouldn't hesitate to go with him to The Ivy. Or anywhere else.

That was the thing with some big lessons. Paul had

clearly been put in her life to show her she wasn't as strong as she'd thought. He'd helped her, really. She'd taken a good, hard look at what she believed in, and she'd made some tough decisions, and she'd never undercut her own power again. The downside was that she'd had to walk through the last of her lesson alone. The man she'd thought was so shallow had turned out to be her teacher. Go figure.

He'd also helped her see that she needed to work out the issues she had with her family before she transferred out of California. That was testing her but good, but it was worth it. She felt a lot less anger at most of her family. Everyone but Autumn, and Gwen wasn't sure that relationship could ever be healed.

"Quit thinking and go," Holly said, giving her a push toward the door.

"I'm going, I'm going. Sheesh."

"Sheesh my big fat behind. Go. Eateth of the popcorn. Drinketh of the soda. Rejoice in the company of a very nice man."

Gwen had to smile. Holly had been nothing but wonderful, despite this whole blind date business. It was good to have friends. Better than good.

Now, all she had to do was make it through the next few hours. She could do it. She was strong. She was invincible.

Oh, who was she kidding. It was going to be a nightmare.

THROUGH NO FAULT of his own, Paul was running late. Two critical meetings had gone long. Then he'd realized he was almost out of gas, the traffic had been worse than usual. He should have walked out of the meeting and damn the consequences.

He yanked his tie off as he hurried toward the bedroom. He'd grab a quick shower. Of all the nights…

Who the hell was at his door? He thought about ignoring the bell, but it rang again. *Damn.* Hurrying, the seconds ticking by too quickly, he flung open the door with a curse ready.

His heart slammed in his chest. Gwen.

"Hey," she said, and in that one word he heard her fear and her hope.

"Hey, yourself."

"I don't really know why I'm here." She looked back toward the street. "I'm supposed to be somewhere else, but…"

"I don't care," he said.

"What?" She turned back to face him. "You don't care that I'm—"

"I don't care why you're here. I'm just so goddamn grateful you are."

Her face changed. It was beautiful before, but with his confession, she became so much more. Her tension fell away and hope filled her eyes. He wanted to kiss her, to hold her tight, to kiss her again and make love to her and the truth was, he couldn't move.

"You are?"

He nodded.

"I was horrible. Stupid. I kicked you out for the worst reasons ever. You were perfect and I was a complete ass."

That made him laugh. "Would you do me a favor?"

She nodded.

"Get in here."

Her smile. It filled him with the kind of happiness that couldn't be studied. The kind that changed a man in every way that mattered.

He pulled her into his arms, heard her purse hit the floor, felt her grab on to his back as if she was never gonna let go.

When he kissed her, everything made sense again.

They stood in the doorway for the longest time. He couldn't get enough of her. Missing her had damn near crippled him and he needed to hold her, taste her, smell her unmistakable, wonderful scent.

Her grip never eased, and when his hand went to her cheek he found it was wet with tears. He wanted to tell her not to cry, but he couldn't stop kissing her even for those few words.

Finally, she was the one who drew back.

"I have so much to apologize for."

"No you don't. It doesn't matter." He meant it. Whatever the reasons, it was over now. She was back. If she only knew how bleak everything had been when he'd lost her, she'd understand.

"Yes, I do. I need to explain what happened."

"Gwen—"

"Please," she said as she stepped to the side. She wiped her face with the back of her hand. "Please."

He closed the front door. "Of course. Tell me everything."

She smiled at him. There was a pretty decent streak of mascara above her cheek, and her lipstick was wonky. It made her even prettier.

"I have to make a phone call first," she said. "I'm supposed to meet someone."

"At the movies?"

"Yeah. How did you—?"

He took her hand in his and led her to the living room. "He knows you can't make it."

She stopped. "What?"

"I was your blind date. Again. This time I wasn't sent by your sister."

Her mouth was open, but no words came out. She stared at him as if she didn't know whether to laugh or cry.

"Holly talked me into it. I was scared to death, but she told me not to be such a wimp."

"Holly?"

"Hey, she's *your* best friend."

"Not anymore."

"Really?"

Gwen took a deep breath. "No, of course not. It was a stupid trick. A perfect trick."

"That's what she said. Not the stupid part."

Gwen went right to his big leather couch and sat down with a thunk. "I… She should have told me. You should have. I almost turned around and drove back to my apartment. Then what would have happened?"

"I'd have come after you. If you weren't ready to see me, I'd have waited. As long as it took."

Gwen took his hand as she scrutinized his face. "How could you still want me after all that happened?"

"How could I not? You destroyed me, kiddo. I couldn't get you out of my head. The more time passed, the worse it got. I was getting desperate. So I called her. Holly."

"The blind date was your idea?"

He gave her what he hoped was a winning smile. "It worked the first time. Holly was the one who gave me hope, though. She said I'd be welcome. And she also told me to make it a movie. I'd wanted to take you dancing."

Gwen blinked. Whimpered just a tiny bit. Whispered, "Oh, my God."

There was no choice but to kiss her again. God, her taste. Her lips, her hair. Her. She'd come back before he'd asked. Before he'd had to beg.

She pulled back, tugging his hands to her lap, holding him still. "Stop taking my breath away, okay? Just for now. I need you to know this. To listen."

He nodded.

She met his gaze clear-eyed and determined. "See, I'd convinced myself that I was this noble person with a great purpose, showing people that obsessing about looks and perfection was foolish and stupid and that anyone who did had to be stupid and foolish and I could write them all off and feel superior." She paused, then continued. "Finally, finally, I stopped thinking about it altogether. I was over it. I was the me I'd always wanted to be.

"And then you came along. I had you pegged from that first moment, but you kept surprising me. You took all my ridiculous assumptions and turned them upside down. Then I got into real trouble when I fell in love with you. Suddenly I was twelve again, being made fun of by all the mean girls in school, and hearing my mother sigh because there was nothing she could do about her unfortunate daughter. Maybe it was because you'd been seeing Autumn, I don't know, but all the issues I'd thought I'd dealt with came back with interest.

"The thing is, I loved you. I just believed you deserved so much more. Eventually, I understood that I deserved more, too."

"You fell in love with me?"

She smiled. "Big-time."

"I had no idea," he said. "It makes sense, though. I've done a lot of soul-searching myself, especially after you and I... It wasn't much fun to admit what an ass I'd been. I was that person you thought I was when we met. What did you say, stupid and foolish?"

"I didn't mean—"

"Yeah, you did. And you were right. I'm still pretty damn amazed that I had enough sense to see something better in me when I had the opportunity." He smiled. "Personally? I think it happened on the dance floor. That very first night. You belonged in my arms. You'll always belong in my arms."

It was clear she was struggling, but he wasn't sure if it was in an effort not to cry or not to speak.

"Because of you," she said, her voice trembling on the edge of tears, "I got to see who I really was. That I hadn't let go of my childhood pain. I was scared, Paul, and it was a child's self-conscious fear. I saw you with my family, and it looked like you fit in so perfectly. Then I got that it was all on the surface. You're nothing like them."

"I wouldn't go that far. I'm still pretty good at being a shallow, selfish bastard."

She shook her head. "Not even close. You're the bravest man I know. You took such a huge chance. You had no idea where it would lead, and yet you kept on going. Look at what you've done. You're who I want to be when I grow up."

He cleared his throat.

"So you know," she said, "I'm working through things with my family. I don't know if I'll end up with any real relationships there, but I'm open. I'd given a lot of thought to moving away, but I tried to follow your example. To stand up and fight for a new life."

He hadn't meant to, but he burst out laughing.

"What's so funny?"

He sighed. "You, trying to be like me. It's official. The whole world's gone mad."

She touched his hair, so lightly he barely felt it. "That's fine with me."

"You know what?" He kissed her nose, then her lips. "I don't really want to go to the movies."

"No?"

"Nope. In fact, I'm thinking I don't want to leave this house until Monday morning. Hmm. Maybe Tuesday. Or Wednesday."

"I can get behind that," she said.

"Unlike you, I'll have to call out for snacks. I don't even have any champagne."

"I don't care. I don't need anything but you." A few seconds passed. Then her smile dimmed. "Well, you and popcorn. I was looking forward to the popcorn."

He had to kiss her again. Which wasn't nearly enough. As he stood, pulling her up with him, he grinned.

"What?" she asked.

"You haven't been here before. I should give you a tour."

She put her arm around his waist. "Sounds terrific."

"I was thinking we'd start with the bedroom."

"Oh?"

"And tomorrow, we'll look at the kitchen."

"Great."

"But there's a lot to see in that bedroom."

She looked up at him with a smile. "I'm all yours."

He sighed as they headed toward his bedroom. She felt so good against him. "Hey, Gwen?"

"Yeah?"

"You know I love you, right?"

Her head fell against his shoulder. "I was hoping."

He pulled her around so he could look into her eyes. "Don't hope. Know. I want you to be with me. Here, at the bar, at whatever parties I can drag you to. I was miserable without you, got it? I don't ever want to go through that again."

Her eyes glistened as she moved closer, as she kissed him.

Somehow, they got to the bedroom. But they missed Monday night trivia, Wednesday night softball. Even two Dodger games.

It was perfect.

* * * * *

Here's a sneak peek at
THE CEO'S CHRISTMAS PROPOSITION,
the first in USA TODAY *bestselling author*
Merline Lovelace's HOLIDAYS ABROAD *trilogy*
coming in November 2008.

American Devon McShay is about to get the
Christmas surprise of a lifetime when she meets
her new client, sexy billionaire Caleb Logan, for
the very first time.

Silhouette

Desire

Available November 2008

Her breath whistled out in a sigh of relief when he exited Customs. Devon recognized him right away from the newspaper and magazine articles her friend and partner Sabrina had looked up during her frantic prep work.

Caleb John Logan, Jr. Thirty-one. Six-two. With jet-black hair, laser-blue eyes and a linebacker's shoulders under his charcoal-gray cashmere overcoat. His jaw-dropping good looks didn't score him any points with Devon. She'd learned the hard way not to trust handsome heartbreakers like Cal Logan.

But he was a client. An important one. And she was willing to give someone who'd served a hitch in the marines before earning a B.S. from the University of Oregon, an MBA from Stanford and his first million at the ripe old age of twenty-six the benefit of the doubt.

Right up until he spotted the hot-pink pashmina, that is.

Devon knew the flash of color was more visible than the sign she held up with his name on it. So she wasn't surprised when Logan picked her out of the crowd and cut in her direction. She'd just plastered on her best businesswoman smile when he whipped an arm around her waist. The next moment she was sprawled against his cashmere-covered chest.

"Hello, brown eyes."

Swooping down, he covered her mouth with his.

Sheer astonishment kept Devon rooted to the spot for a few seconds while her mind whirled chaotically. Her first thought was that her client had downed a few too many drinks during the long flight. Her second, that he'd mistaken the kind of escort and consulting services her company provided. Her third shoved everything else out of her head.

The man could kiss!

His mouth moved over hers with a skill that ignited sparks at a half dozen flash points throughout her body. Devon hadn't experienced that kind of spontaneous combustion in a while. A *long* while.

The sparks were still popping when she pushed off his chest, only now they fueled a flush of anger.

"Do you always greet women you don't know with a lip-lock, Mr. Logan?"

A smile crinkled the skin at the corners of his eyes. "As a matter of fact, I don't. That was from Don."

"Huh?"

"He said he owed you one from New Year's Eve two years ago and made me promise to deliver it."

She stared up at him in total incomprehension. Logan hooked a brow and attempted to prompt a nonexistent memory.

"He abandoned you at the Waldorf. Five minutes before midnight. To deliver twins."

"I don't have a clue who or what you're..."

Understanding burst like a water balloon.

"Wait a sec. Are you talking about Sabrina's old boyfriend? Your buddy, who's now an ob-gyn doc?"

It was Logan's turn to look startled. He recovered faster than Devon had, though. His smile widened into a rueful grin.

"I take it you're not Sabrina Russo."

"No, Mr. Logan, I am *not*."

* * * * *

Be sure to look for
THE CEO'S CHRISTMAS PROPOSITION
by Merline Lovelace.
Available in November 2008
wherever books are sold,
including most bookstores, supermarkets,
drugstores and discount stores.

nocturne™

ESCAPE THE CHILL OF WINTER WITH TWO SPECIAL STORIES FROM BESTSELLING AUTHORS

MICHELE HAUF

AND

VIVI ANNA

WINTER KISSED

In "A Kiss of Frost," photographer Kate Wilson experiences the icy kisses of Jal Frosti, but soon learns that this icy god has a deadly ulterior motive. Can Kate's love melt his heart?

In "Ice Bound," Dr. Darien Calder travels to the north island of Japan, where he discovers an icy goddess who is rumored to freeze doomed travelers. Darien is determined to melt her beautiful but frosty exterior and break her of the curse she carries...before it's too late.

Available November wherever books are sold.

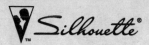

REQUEST YOUR FREE BOOKS!

2 FREE NOVELS PLUS 2 FREE GIFTS!

HARLEQUIN®

Blaze™

Red-hot reads!

HARLEQUIN®

Blaze™

COMING NEXT MONTH

#429 KISS & TELL Alison Kent
In the world of celebrity tabloids, Caleb MacGregor is the best. Once he smells a scandal, he makes sure the world knows. And that's exactly what Miranda Kelly is afraid of. Hiding behind her stage name, Miranda hopes she'll avoid his notice. And she does—until she invites Caleb into her bed.

#430 UNLEASHED Lori Borrill
It's a wild ride in more ways than one when Jessica Beane is corralled into a road trip by homicide detective Rick Marshall. Crucial evidence is missing and Jess is the key to unlocking not just the case, but their pent-up passion, as well!

#431 A BODY TO DIE FOR Kimberly Raye
Love at First Bite, Bk. 3
Vampire Viviana Darland is in Skull Creek, Texas, looking for one thing—an orgasm. Or more specifically, the only man who's ever given her one, vampire Garret Sawyer. She knows her end is near, and wants one good climax before she goes. And she intends to get it—before Garret delivers on his promise to kill her....

#432 HER SEXIEST SURPRISE Dawn Atkins
He's the best birthday gift ever! When Chloe Baxter makes a sexy wish on her birthday candles, she never expects Riley Connelly—her secret crush—to appear. Nor does she expect him to give her the hottest night of her life. It's so hot, why share just one night?

#433 RECKLESS Tori Carrington
Indecent Proposals, Bk. 1
Heidi Joblowski isn't a woman to leave her life to chance. Her plan? To marry her perfect boyfriend, Jesse, and have several perfect children. Unfortunately, the only perfect thing in her life lately is the sex she's been having with Jesse's best friend Kyle....

#434 IN A BIND Stephanie Bond
Sex for Beginners, Bk. 2
Flight attendant Zoe Smythe is working her last shift, planning her wedding... and doing her best to ignore the sexual chemistry between her and a seriously sexy Australian passenger. But when she reads a letter she'd written in college, reminding her of her most private, erotic fantasies...all bets are off!

www.eHarlequin.com

HBCNM1008BPA